STONES OF FIRE

JERIS HAMM

ILLUSTRATED BY JOEL COCKRELL

CANDLE TREE
PRESS

Stones of Fire
© 2025 by Jeris Hamm
Cover and interior art copyright © 2025 Joel Cockrell
Some interior illustrations © 2023 Brandon Dorman

Published by Candle Tree Press, LLC, 4161 River Links Dr., Spring Hill, TN.

Printed in the United States of America

Summary: Young teen Matt Silvers must recapture the Stones of Fire and rescue the Guardian, Jasper, from the clutches of the evil Wolvin. As a Valenian protégé, Matt travels to Scotland and battles Druid thieves while his best friend, Ryan, must escape the paralyzing grip of the Rim. Meanwhile, in his hometown of Baywood, his friend, Julie, faces lizard invaders from the Dark Void.

ISBN: 979-8-9872156-6-1 (hardcover) / ISBN 979-8-9872156-4-7 (pb) / ISBN 979-8-9872156-5-4 (electronic book)

CONTENTS

Peeps and Plots .... *vii*

Chapter One: Bullies *1*

Chapter Two: Good Move? *7*

Chapter Three: Relics *13*

Chapter Four: Whoosh *23*

Chapter Five: Revenge *33*

Chapter Six: Slizard *41*

Chapter Seven: Flying Solo *43*

Chapter Eight: Captured *51*

Chapter Nine: Secret Chauffeur *55*

Chapter Ten: Fury *63*

Chapter Eleven: Wickety and Wavy *67*

Chapter Twelve: Telling Tales *75*

Chapter Thirteen: Anxious Arrival *81*

Chapter Fourteen: The Hidden Den *91*

Chapter Fifteen: The Creepy Cone *105*

Chapter Sixteen: The Rim *115*

Chapter Seventeen: Deep Dive *121*

Chapter Eighteen: The Valenians *129*

Chapter Nineteen: Dawdle *135*

Chapter Twenty: The Lost One *141*

Chapter Twenty-One: Discovery *149*

Chapter Twenty-Two: Predator *157*

Chapter Twenty-Three: Bonfire *167*

Chapter Twenty-Four: Lizardville *173*

Chapter Twenty-Five: Enemies 179
Chapter Twenty-Six: Attack Plan 183
Chapter Twenty-Seven: Warrior Princess 193
Chapter Twenty-Eight: Flash and a Clash 199
Chapter Twenty-Nine: Into the Light 207
Chapter Thirty: The Prism Bridge 215
Chapter Thirty-One: Homeward 227
Chapter Thirty-Two: Hiss 233
Epilogue 241

In Appreciation 247

PEEPS AND PLOTS

FROM

The Secret of the Seven Rubies
(BOOK #1 IN THE TIME TREADERS SERIES)

Meet the Peeps

(Introduced by the author, but the characters kind of take over)

In Baywood:

Matt Silvers

Matt Silvers is in the eighth grade at Baywood Junior High. He's average height, but short for a basketball player. His dusty brown hair sticks up and his left eye twitches when he's stressed out. He does okay in school, but he's not an Einstein. He is sometimes late to school and doesn't always finish his homework. Matt has a Shar-Pei dog (Wrinkles) and a dirt bike. Matt has certain "abilities" that are unveiled during his quests as a Valenian, and he is learning how to use them.

Best moment(s): Journeying to the realm of Koinopia with the wise Guardian, Jasper. Being initiated into the tribe of the Valenians. Hanging out with his best friends, Ryan and Julie. And, whoa, making it to the basketball championship game and playing against Westside.

Worst moment: Battling the evil Craevin invaders who set a dangerous trap for his grandfather and mesmerized his friends with an evil video game.

Ryan Davis

Ryan is taller than Matt and is a starter on the basketball team. He loves to eat, especially sweets. Ryan has a "hover mother," but she's trusting him a little more. Ryan stumbles into trouble and stresses out, but in the end, he often saves the day. Ryan likes to use "Z" words and lives close to Julie Spencer.

Best moment(s): His journeys with Matt to Koinopia. Hanging with Matt after school. Eating his mom's double-chocolate peanut butter pie. And whenever the Baywood Hawks basketball team has a win!

Worst moment(s): Being zonked by the evil Starblades video game. Whenever there is a math test, he breaks out in a rash. Getting lost on a four-wheeler trail one time and having a flat tire. And it was raining.

Julie Spencer

Julie is a star player on the girls' basketball team. She's a good student and loves animals—maybe someday she'll be a vet. She likes to draw with glitter pens and make jewelry. She usually wears her sandy-blonde hair in a ponytail, but some of her friends say it looks cool when she wears a couple of braids. She likes to

challenge the boys in sports. Ryan is her neighbor, and she and Matt have become good friends.

Best moment(s): Traveling to Koinopia with Jasper and meeting the Butterlings. Hugs from her little sister Millie. Making the most baskets during the hot shot competition. The awesome Baywood Hawks playing Westside for the championship!

Worst moment(s): When she accused her little sister of ruining her stuff. When just about the whole school was hypnotized by the evil Starblades game. When she put colored streaks in her hair, and it turned her whole hair blue! Standing at the free-throw line and missing both shots.

Paige Silvers

Paige Silvers is Matt's mom. She's pretty and smart. She loves numbers and works with Matt's father at Quantum. Matt thinks she wants to have a food truck because she's always trying out recipes and has fancy kitchen stuff in the garage. She works in their home office and always asks Matt how he's doing. Her father is an adventurer (Matt's Grandpa).

Best moment(s): Meeting Ben and having Matt. Quantum being saving from video game thieves. Winning a blue ribbon for her strawberry tarts. Adding up numbers correctly is cool, too.

Worst moment: Whenever someone she loves gets hurt.

Ben Silvers

Ben Silvers is Matt's father. He has dark hair and can be kind of nerdy, but he's chilling. He and Matt's mother own a computer game company called Quantum. Ben attends all of Matt's ball games, except when company stuff sometimes keeps him away. He has lots of awards and watches over his family and his business. When Matt thinks his dad is clueless, his father surprises him by knowing a lot of things.

Best moment(s): Meeting Paige and holding Matt for the first time. Saving Quantum.

Worst moment(s): If there is ever a time he can't protect his family. When his company doesn't do well.

Grandpa

Grandpa is Matt's grandfather. He fought in a couple of wars and goes on a lot of adventures. He travels into the mountains and the wilderness. Grandpa has a gray ponytail and uses herbs for medicine. He won't back down from a fight, and he's taught Matt how to protect himself. Grandpa is tough and drives an old Jeep—it's usually crusted with dirt. Matt's mom worries about him because he is not as young as he used to be and gets sick sometimes.

Best moment: Returning home to his family after the wars.

Worst moment(s): Falling into the basement at the old train depot. After the war, being thousands of miles away from home and wondering if he would ever get back

Wrinkles

Matt's Shar Pei dog and confidant. Wrinkles delivered one of the seven rubies to Matt, wearing it on his collar. Likes to jump on Matt's bed, but sometimes misses. Meets Matt at the school bus stop when school is over.

From the Kingdom of Koinopia:

The Eternal One

One whose presence is everywhere. The Kingdom is filled with His Light. The Eternal One is ultimate good and truth, who guides, protects, and calls Earth people into His Kingdom.

Jasper

Jasper is an other-worldly warrior who guards the realm of Koinopia. Almost seven feet tall, he has emerald eyes and dark hair. He chooses earthly partners to take part in his quests. Jasper

oversees Matt's training as a Valenian. Jasper battles alongside the Valenians and other beings of light to fight evil on every side. He often wears armor but may appear in magnificent robes or even in simple human covering. He wants only good for the people of earth (Earples) and desires wisdom to triumph. He lives in a crystal undersea cavern but appears in the earthly realm.

Best moment(s): Every moment in Koinopia, although there is no time there. No one is in a hurry and life just is. On Earth, the best moments are when evil is driven back and good triumphs.

Worst moment: When the first man and first woman on Earth made a really bad choice and listened to a snake.

The Valenians

A Robin Hood-like tribe who protect the borderlands of Koinopia. They are medieval warriors who battle the forces of evil that invade from the Dark Void. Noris, Juman, and others are ready for battle at every turn. They initiated Matt into their tribe after his first victory over the Craevin and the Dark Void. Petrus is their leader.

Petrus

Tall and muscular, Petrus is the Prince of the Woodlands and the leader of the Valenians. His blonde hair and good humor disguise his warrior toughness.

The Pellegrin

Avian creatures from Koinopia with red or silver wings who travel between realms. They fight off the forces of darkness. They are couriers of the ancient red chest—a portal between Koinopia and Earth. The Pellegrin delivered the chest and the first ruby to Matt from the Crystal  Cavern, where Jasper resides. They retrieved the chest after Matt's victory over the Craevin and journeyed back toward Koinopia.

The Butterlings

Butterfly-like creatures who swirl around Koinopia, displaying their rainbow colors and helping Jasper and the Earples (Earth people) seeking to enter the Kingdom.

Stubley

A creature of the Living Waters in Koinopia who appears as a cross between a dolphin and walrus. He escorts Matt and his friends through the deep waters to Jasper's Crystal Cavern.

Golden Winged Woman

A creature with lacy wings who appears to Matt, Julie, and Ryan as they travel the Winding Pathway in Koinopia. She gives them a message from Jasper.

Others (Creeps, *Not* Peeps)

Wesley

A bully at school with red hair and big arms. After first making fun of Matt and the basketball team, Wes finally came around to their side. Sort of. Wes just got a pet chameleon that he keeps in his garage.

Needles

New kid that uses his smarts, but not in a nice way. Could be a peep, but hangs with Wesley and annoys Matt. His father was a turncoat employee at Quantum and tried to steal the Silvers' video game, Starblazers.

The Gridleys

Needles' family including his stepdad and brothers that cause Matt trouble. Definitely not peeps.

Slag and the Craevin

Beetle-like creatures sent from the Dweller of the Dark Void who schemed against Matt and the town of Baywood to bring chaos and confusion. They failed. Worse than creeps. Slag is their leader.

The Dweller of the Dark Void

Evil being that sends chaos and confusion, sadness and death into the Earth realm. The mesmerizing Dark Void is the Dweller's domain. The Dweller is constantly scheming against those who stand with the Eternal One and against evil. The Dweller sent the evil Craevin into Baywood.

CHAPTER ONE

BULLIES

"**G**et out of my way!" A shrill voice cut through the usual chatter of the junior high hallway.

Matt Silvers stopped mid-stride, squeaking his tennis shoes on the waxed floor. "You hear that?" He held back his best friend, Ryan Davis. "That sounds like Julie."

"Yeah." Ryan's eyes widened.

Matt turned and sped down the hall toward Julie Spencer's locker. Ryan jogged beside him as they passed the science lab. Matt waved away the stinky fumes that drifted out of the lab and turned a corner into a section of blue lockers. It was Julie, all right. And Wesley Norman blocked her way.

"Come on, Julie!" Wes edged closer. "I just need your notes from science class." He folded his arms. "Plus your homework."

"No way!" Julie stood tall, her blonde ponytail bobbing as she shook her head. Her arms encircled her notebook.

Matt, then Ryan, placed themselves between Wes and Julie.

"Back off, Wesley." Matt stared up at Baywood Junior High's worst bully and didn't like the look on his face. Wes had recently shaved his red hair into a crewcut. And his lack of deodorant didn't win him any new friends. Word around the school was that Wes kept a pet chameleon in a cage at home. It might be cool, but also kind of creepy.

"Yeah Wes, don't you have to be somewhere else about now?" Ryan said. "I think I saw your pet lizard escaping down the hallway. Better slither after him."

Wesley tilted his head and squinted. "Funny, Davis."

"I thought so." Julie laughed and so did Matt. A crowd gathered around them.

Wesley's chin dropped a few inches, and his shoulders lowered. "Nothing wrong with asking for a little help."

"You're right, Mr. Norman." Principal Harris's voice cut through the crowd. He stood just behind them, a foot taller than the group. "There's nothing wrong with asking for help. But when you asked for her homework—that's different." He shook his head. "And the way you stood over her—I'd consider it bullying."

Wesley's head dropped further. "I was just kidding."

"Not funny, Wes," Matt added.

"All you students get to class." Mr. Harris stood with his hands on his hips, his broad shoulders stretching his white shirt, his navy tie hanging perfectly straight. The students dispersed, and the principal pointed Wesley toward the office. Wesley obeyed, his eyes narrowing into slits. Principal Harris followed at his heels.

Matt turned to Julie. "You okay?"

"Yeah—what's up with Wes anyway?" She slid her glittered purse onto her shoulder and zipped the books inside her bag.

"When he helped us celebrate the basketball team's championship, I thought he'd changed."

Ryan watched Wes skulk away. "Maybe he's like his pet chameleon—always changing, and you never know what to expect."

"Yeah." Matt nodded to his friends as they separated and headed toward the library. He skimmed past the glassed-in front of the principal's office. Mr. Harris spoke into his phone, probably talking to Wes's parents.

Wes sat in a yellow chair just outside the office. The elementary school chair was too small for him.

"Wait until you need some help, Silvers," Wes grumbled. "You won't be laughing then."

"Yeah? When would that be?" Matt halted.

"I noticed you're not going out for the baseball team. Afraid you're not tough enough to join?"

Matt's eye twitched. Wesley knew how to push all the wrong buttons.

Matt's last baseball game in the sixth grade had not been a good one. He'd been hit in the head by a wild pitch. Was he too scared to try again?

Mr. Harris appeared in the doorway. "Wesley? Come in here a minute."

Matt exhaled and walked on. He wouldn't answer Wes. Would he ever give up his bullying ways?

But even Wes's attitude couldn't dim Matt's memory of the day his basketball team won the district trophy.

His team had arrived back at school after the win to find the band playing their school song while the students and parents cheered. Navy blue streamers and gold balloons hung everywhere. Pizza and cupcakes made it that much better. It was the best day of junior high so far. Even now, the first week of March, some tournament-week posters still decorated the halls—Hawks #1!

And then there was the Monday after the championship game. The morning Matt had learned that a certain battle *off* the basketball court hadn't ended.

A good day had taken a scary turn. One minute he was standing in his driveway before school and the next minute, the world around him dissolved and the forestland of the Valenians sprung up around him.

Matt had accepted a challenge to join the Valenians and their quests, but the Robin Hood-like tribe wasn't of the earthly realm—their home was the Woodlands surrounding Koinopia. They had appeared to Matt that day and drawn him into their realm for a special initiation.

But the welcoming ceremony stalled when the evil Wolvin attacked, catching them unaware, chasing them through the woods, and shooting flaming arrows. Matt and the Valenians had narrowly escaped.

Matt's hurried initiation finally took place inside an earthen hideout. And just as quickly as he'd entered the Woodlands of Koinopia, he'd returned to the realm of time where his home, family, and best dog Wrinkles lived.

Matt shook off the memory of the Wolvin as he strode down the school ramp toward study hall. His hand went to the leather necklace under his shirt, and he rolled it between his fingers. A pure white stone hung in the middle of the strand, a badge of honor from the Valenians.

The Valenians hadn't contacted him since the day of his initiation. Had the Wolvin overtaken them? What about the mighty Guardian, Jasper? Matt grasped the stone now and closed his eyes.

Jasper, where are you?

Although his training with Jasper had been tough, Matt knew he'd grown in his special abilities and strength. Even standing up to Wes's bullying hadn't scared him.

Sometimes Matt got so caught up in school drama and hanging out on the weekends that days would go by when he didn't think about Jasper, the Valenians, or the quest for the seven rubies.

He, Ryan, and Julie had discovered four rubies and the messages of secret wisdom that came with them. They'd used wisdom to defeat the evil Craevin.

But three rubies remained to be found, like golden tickets to Koinopia. Without them, the secret kingdom seemed like a far-away dream.

And Matt didn't have a clue where to find them.

Jasper, where are you?

Jasper's eyes flew open. Sleep brought his only escape. The icy dungeon of his imprisonment grew colder every minute. He curled deeper into his woolen cloak. He was sure he'd heard Matt's voice, but how could he get a message to him?

Jasper had been caught off guard. He'd entered the Earth realm weeks ago to celebrate Matt's victory over the Craevin. They'd watched together as the Craevin hordes had been blasted back into lower Earth, and they knew the battle had been won. The happy day, the beautiful sunshine, and the soft breezes had softened Jasper's defenses.

Moments after leaving Matt, the Wolvin attacked. They had lured Jasper into a trap and thrown a net of heavy iron over his head. The new enemy sent from the Dark Void attacked in vicious, wolf-like, and lightning-fast movements. How could Jasper have been so careless?

He needed Matt's help.

The Valenians had welcomed the young teenager into their tribe. The Eternal One had chosen Matt Silvers to live in a particular place at precisely this time. He was the seventh generation of the Silvers family, a heritage of renown. Matt had entered his training as a Valenian and had won his first battle against darkness.

The unveiling of his special abilities had given him courage. Matt had risen to the challenge of his first training, but what would happen now?

The mighty Guardian sat up. If only he could reach out to the young Valenian. Matt had advanced, but the gift of extraordinary hearing had yet to be given.

Jasper rested his back against the icy wall. He cupped his hands and blew into them, trying to release some warmth.

If Matt were a Koinopian, reaching out to him with words would be easy. But—

A sea of faces entered Jasper's mind. He could reach out to one of his Koinopian friends and send a message to Matt through one of them.

One woman stood out from the rest. She enjoyed the beauty of Earth and often visited. If she were there now, she could give Matt a message.

Jasper winced at the shackles around his wrist. The cuffs had been cruelly fashioned by the powers of the Dark Void and could be removed in only one way.

The Stones of Fire would disintegrate them!

It was Jasper's hope of escape. Matt must find the Stones of Fire and somehow bring them to this dreary place. The way would be difficult and dangerous.

A fire of hope ignited in Jasper's heart as he prayed for his young friend's strength.

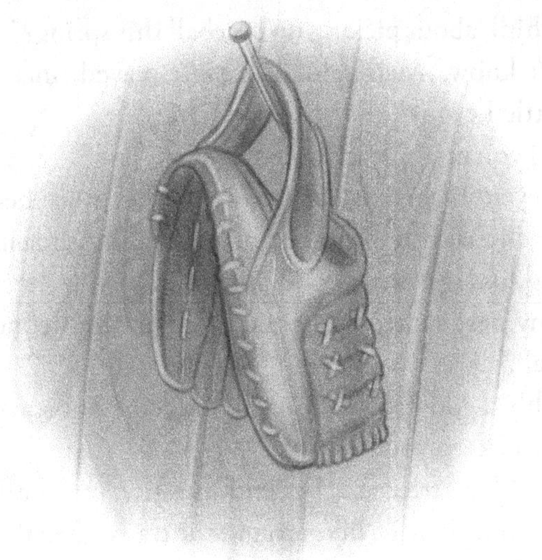

CHAPTER TWO

GOOD MOVE?

Coach Bryson stood at the front of the classroom, his wide frame almost blocking out the homework assignment he'd written on the whiteboard.

He wore a navy polo shirt with a Baywood Hawks logo and "Coach of the Year" embroidered underneath. The basketball team had given it to him it as a thank-you for a winning season.

Matt finished copying the assignment just as the dismissal tone buzzed. He gathered his books and headed for the door.

"Matt?" Coach raised a brow and called him back. "Got a minute?"

Matt stopped and stepped to Coach's desk. "Yes, sir?"

Matt respected Coach in the classroom just like the other teachers, although he knew Coach better than the rest. He had become Matt's mentor during the season.

7

"Ever think about picking up baseball this spring?"

"I don't know," Matt said. "I haven't played since the sixth grade in Little League."

"How'd you do?" Coach asked.

Matt's eye twitched. It had been two years since he'd played. The wild pitch that had blackened his eye and the slide into home that skinned his leg weren't good memories.

"Not my best sport," Matt said. "That's why I concentrated on basketball."

"Probably a good move." Coach nodded. "But staying active this spring will keep you in shape."

"Yeah." Matt tried to be enthusiastic, but he'd already dreamed of riding his dirt bike around the trails when the weather got warm. "What's up, Coach?"

"We're starting a team, and I need two more players." Coach sighed. "I'll be straight. We need this baseball team to help the school receive a grant. It's money that can be used for all the programs—including basketball.

"We've got a practice tonight. Why don't you join us? Let me know what you think in a couple of days."

Matt nodded. "I'll think about it."

◇◇◇◇

Matt stepped off the school bus into the late afternoon light. Shafts of sunlight filtered inside his garage and rested on Matt's old baseball glove, hanging from a nail. His father was in the garage, looking over his golf clubs.

"Hey, Dad," Matt said. "Coach asked me about playing baseball today at school."

Dad stopped and turned toward him. "Baseball? I didn't think you were still interested. It's been a few years."

"Yeah—Little League. But Coach needs a couple of more players to form a team. He said it has something to do with a grant."

"Ah." Dad set down the golf bag. "I'm not sure if that's a good reason to join."

"I'd probably be low on the roster," Matt added. "But at least Coach would have the players he needs."

"He *has* done a lot for you boys," Dad said. "But are you sure you'd want to devote that much time to playing?"

"It would keep me in shape for high school basketball tryouts. Coach invited me to practice tonight."

Dad nodded. "If you want to go, I'll take you to practice. Then you can decide if you want to join the team."

◊◊◊◊

A cool wind blew across the lawn leading to Baywood Junior High's baseball field. Matt zipped up his hoodie and jogged across the damp soil. New grass rose from the ground, along with the smell of blooming buttercups. It had been a while since he'd attended a spring practice. He'd forgotten how cold it could be at the beginning of the season.

Sand collected on his shoes as he stepped onto the diamond. Lights flickered on, and Matt spied some familiar faces. Jake and Austin threw the ball to each other, warming up. Parker and Lucas stood in left field, stopping the ground balls Coach sent their way. Caleb and Colin ran the bases and practiced sliding into home.

There were even some girls watching practice from the bleachers. Julie sat there with some cool freshman girls from the high school—Jennifer and Abby.

Matt approached the dugout.

"What are you doing here?" Wesley bellowed as he laced up his cleats.

"Yeah, Silvers. Didn't you hurt your ankle during the basketball championship? Or were you just faking?" Needles stood outside the fence surrounding the dugout. Although he didn't actually play, he kept stats for the team.

Matt had tried to avoid Baywood's know-it-all student. Needles had tried to upload a pirated video game to the internet.

The game belonged to Quantum—the company owned by Matt's parents. But Needles and his stepfather had tried to steal it.

Matt returned his attention to the guys warming up. Caleb slid into home and jogged toward the dugout. Matt gave the seventh-grader a five as he passed by.

Wesley stood and came over to Matt. "Thought you'd be too chicken to show up," he said, crossing his arms.

"Matt's no chicken," Caleb said. "Made the winning basket for the championship. Even with a hurt ankle."

"Dude, that's awesome." A new player Matt didn't know spoke up from the bench. The guy had sandy blonde hair and an accent, not exactly from Tennessee.

"Coach asked me to come," Matt said, ignoring the digs. He'd learned to let some things go—overcome evil with good.

Maybe Wes would back off. Jasper had told him that changes in Wes's life would take time. The same for Needles.

If only Ryan were here. But Matt knew if he joined the baseball team, he'd be playing with different guys.

Coach waved Parker and Lucas in, then headed to the dugout. He lifted a clipboard from a nail on a wooden post. He glanced at the paper, then at the players.

His gaze rested on Matt. "Glad to see you joined us. Along with Wyatt, that gives us enough for a team."

Matt nodded.

"Okay, guys. I'm dividing you up. Half in the outfield, half batting." Coach separated the team members. He looked over his glasses at Matt. "You're with the batting group."

Great. I haven't batted in two years.

Coach called out the batting lineup. "Silvers, you're last."

Matt lifted his head. That was fine with him, especially since Wesley was pitching.

The team members at-bat before him did okay. They hit a few doubles and singles. Then came Matt's turn. He slapped on a helmet and picked up a bat; he wouldn't give in to fear. Matt walked to home plate, lifted his bat, and turned to face Wesley.

A grin spread across Wesley's face. He rubbed the ball as if he were heating it up. Wesley grunted as he wound up, then shot the ball in Matt's direction. The ball came in fast, and Matt jumped back. It'd almost hit him in the shins.

"Wesley! Focus those pitches!" Coach hollered from the fence.

Wesley's next two pitches were balls, and Matt swung at the third. He hit it, but the ball barely made it over second base. Jake made an easy catch in the outfield.

Wesley laughed. "Ohh . . . power hitter."

Needles chimed in as Matt came into the dugout to get his glove. "Way to go, loser."

Matt shook his head. "It's only a practice game, Needles. Chill."

The new guy, Wyatt, joined in. "Yeah, dude. What's your problem?"

Matt's group took the field. Coach positioned Matt in the outfield, between second and third base.

Lucas pitched, and only one hit made it past the infield. Parker scooped it up and threw it to first for an out. Then Colin tagged a guy headed to second. Wesley batted next.

"Better back up," Austin called to Matt from right field.

Matt nodded. He knew Wesley could throw all his weight into hitting the ball, and his strong arms usually sent it toward the fence.

Lucas threw two strikes across the plate, and Wesley sent the next pitch sailing. It flew high over the infield and into left field.

Matt glanced up. The ball came fast—right toward him. His glove felt stiff on his hand, from all those months in the garage. He opened his glove and looked up. The ball headed toward his glove—then hit the top and glanced off, hitting Matt in the forehead.

The edges of his vision turned gray. He stumbled and took a few steps. All of a sudden, everything went black.

C H A P T E R T H R E E

RELICS

Matt felt something cold on his forehead. He opened his eyes. Dad knelt next to him, and Coach on the other side.

"Matt." Dad patted his cheek. "Are you with us?"

He blinked. "Yeah." He squinted. "What happened?"

"Ball bounced and hit your forehead," Coach shook his head. "Sorry this happened during the first practice."

Dad removed the ice pack from Matt's head, and he sat up. Some of the team had gathered around him. His head throbbed, but he thought he'd be okay. "I'm all right."

Dad offered his hand. Matt took it and stood.

Coach scooted his cap back and scratched his head. "Why don't you call it a night? You probably need to have that checked out."

"We're parked close by," Dad said. "Think you can make it?"

Matt nodded.

He wouldn't look at Wesley or Needles. It would be bad enough when he saw them at school tomorrow.

"Take care, dude," Wyatt said and opened the fence gate for Matt. The girls watching practice stood close by. Matt's cheeks warmed. The high school girls had seen him at his worst. What would they think of him next year when he was a freshman?

◇◇◇◇

During school on Tuesday, Matt tried to avoid Wesley and Needles. But Needles was in one of his afternoon classes. Sure enough, as he headed for history, Needles met him in the hallway, heading in the opposite direction.

"Hey, Silvers. You're headed in the wrong direction," Needles said. "Guess that knot on your forehead affected your brain. Can't you remember *anything*?" He snickered. "Our history class is in the library today." Needles bumped his shoulder as he walked past.

"Yeah, whatever," Matt said and stopped.

Matt *almost* felt sorry for him. But not really. Needles bragged every time he made an "A"—usually a 100, in class.

Matt turned around and headed to the library. As he entered, soft carpet quieted his steps, and the smell of dusty books drifted to him. Metal bookshelves stood on each side of a wood-floored area surrounding the librarian's desk. To his left, dust-speckled light filtered through the windows onto the long library tables.

His friend Bailey Price sat at the end of one of the tables, thumbing through a big book. Matt stopped in front of him.

"Hey, Price. Why the huge book?"

"It's history. Before the internet. Cool pictures."

"Yeah?" Matt sat to one side.

Bailey pointed to a large illustration in the book. The muted colors looked like a medieval painting taken from an ancient castle.

"The hills of Scotland," Bailey explained. "Home of the bagpipes." He honked out a few musical notes, imitating a bagpipe.

Matt laughed, then studied the two-page illustration. Tall mountains surrounded wildflower meadows with emerald grass—so green it looked unreal. And the sky reflected the shimmering lakes and the deep blue of the ocean. Misty clouds shadowed ghostly gray bluffs.

"That's cool," Matt said. He peered closer, and the picture drew him in. He could feel the wind blowing down the steep cliffs and the sun warming his face. A warm, sweet flower scent tickled his nose.

His Valenian senses kicked in. Was this intuition or beyond-seeing? Maybe a combination of both. Or some new Valenian strength. His eyes swept from the ocean to the rocky crags.

"Matt, hello! Are you still with me?" Bailey studied Matt like a captured bug.

"Yeah." Matt raised his head and blinked at his friend, bringing Bailey's face into focus.

"You're really zoned out," Bailey said.

Matt shook his head. "That's an awesome picture. I felt like I was inside it."

Bailey nodded but quirked an eyebrow. He rolled his wheelchair away from the table. "Got to head to the band room. Later, Matt."

"Yeah, later."

After Bailey left the library, Matt shut the massive book and studied the cover. The title wasn't written in English.

"Matt Silvers, isn't it?"

Matt flinched. Miss Duncan had come over to stand beside the table. The new librarian insisted on quiet. She wore her light hair in a bun, and a red plaid scarf had been tied at her neck.

"Yes, ma'am."

"Quite an interesting book, I'd say." Her brows rose above her black glasses.

"Yeah." Matt pointed at the title. "What's this language?"

Miss Duncan peered over her spectacles. "It is Gaelic."

The unfamiliar words nearly took up the whole cover: *Ionmhas na Gaidhealtachd.*

The librarian squinted. "I can give you a translation."

"Miss Duncan?" A student called from the librarian's desk, waiting to be checked out.

"One moment, Matt." She returned to the check-out area but glanced in Matt's direction.

While Miss Duncan helped the other student, Matt leafed through the pages following the illustration. The funny writing continued inside, with drawings of marshy bogs and old castles, spooky dark clouds, and . . . what's this? A fireplace hearth in a room with a low ceiling and a large, wood-carved chair. An animal-skin rug. And a low table with a candle, a wooden helmet, and . . . a red chest.

Matt turned the book and brought it closer. Could it be? He lowered his head. It was the red chest from Koinopia! *Whoa.* And it had four rubies sitting on top! He closed the book a little too hard.

"Don't be giving up on the book yet." Miss Duncan walked over and pointed at the words on the cover. "I think you'll be intrigued by the title. It says, 'Treasure of the Highlands.'"

Matt's head buzzed. He slid back in his chair.

"Something wrong?" Miss Duncan asked.

"Thanks for your help, but I better join my class." Matt's heart pounded.

"Oh, yes. Your history class is meeting in the conference room."

Matt nodded and glanced toward an enclosed area of the library.

"This book can't be checked out, you know," Miss Duncan said. "I'll place it back on the 900s shelf so you know where to find it." She peered sideways at him. "Whenever you're ready."

Matt nodded and strode through the library to join his class. What did it mean? Maybe he could catch Ryan and Julie before the school day ended. The three of them could figure it out together.

◇◇◇◇

Matt waited outside the keyboarding class for Ryan. Ryan came through and stopped just outside the room, checking out their friend Parker's new graphic novel.

"Yeah man, that's cool." Ryan stood taller than the group he was with, and his dark skin seemed to glow under his gold Baywood Hawks T-shirt.

"Hey, Ryan." Matt touched his elbow.

Ryan turned. "Matt?" He waved to the group, and they walked on. He crinkled his brows. "Hey, what's up?"

"There's something strange in the library."

"Man—let me guess. The zoology books again? Checking out the family tree?"

Matt smirked. "Funny."

Julie came around the corner. "Oh, you two. By the way, thanks for the save."

"No problem. But you were standing up to Wes pretty well on your own," Matt said.

"It never hurts to have your friends helping out." A smile touched Julie's mouth.

Matt motioned Ryan and Julie toward a corner. "I saw the red chest."

"What? Where?" Ryan asked. "I thought the Pellegrin took the chest back to Koinopia."

"Well, I saw it. In this really old book in the library," Matt said. "An illustration inside of it."

"How do you know it's the same chest?" Julie asked.

"The four rubies on top. They were placed beneath a golden wreath—just like we last saw it." Matt sighed. "I know it's the same one."

Ryan frowned. "You had the red chest just a few weeks ago. How can it be in a book that is way older than we are? There's like zero chance it's the same one."

"I know." Matt rested his back against the hallway's block wall and folded his arms.

"I've got study hall in the library now," Julie said. "I'll check it out."

"Miss Duncan knows where it is," Matt said. "Just ask for the book with the Gaelic writing."

✧✧✧✧

In the library, Julie sat and opened her Tennessee history book. She flipped through the pages of times past—Fort Nashborough, Andrew Jackson, the Mississippi River cotton trade, and the historical roots of all kinds of music.

"Hey, Julie."

Julie looked up. Two girls from her basketball team—Dillon and Darby, stood in front of her table. They weren't twins, but they were always together.

"Just came in with our English class," Dillon said. "Returning our books."

"Hey, way to make Wes back down," Darby added.

"Shh." Julie spoke in a low voice. "I didn't do it alone." She motioned for her friends to sit across from her. "Besides, I'd rather forget the whole thing."

A deeper voice came from behind her. "Yeah. Wes was totally not cool."

Julie turned. A tall guy with blond, messy-fringed bangs stood beside her. Her pulse beat a little faster. He must be a new student.

"You know Wes?"

"Don't know him too well yet. But he's on the baseball team with me." He pulled out a chair, turned it backward, and straddled it. His dark-brown eyes glanced at her book. "You're in Mr. Benson's history class, right?"

"Um . . ." Julie hesitated. Across from her, Dillon elbowed Darby. Darby raised her eyebrows and smiled.

The guy grinned. "I thought I saw you. Think you might help me out in that class? Promise I won't bother you like Wes."

Julie found her voice. "Sure—I guess. It would help if I knew your name."

"Yeah, that." He laughed. "I'm Wyatt Sawyer." Wyatt became serious. "This baseball team is important to me. Got to keep my grades up."

"Maybe I can help you during study hall," Julie said.

"Awesome!" Wyatt's eyes lit up. He smacked the table with his hand. "Thanks." He left the girls and joined some guys at the computers.

"I wonder how much work you'll get done?" Darby laughed.

"*Please.*" Julie scooted back her chair. She had to find the Gaelic book before study hall ended. "I've gotta look for something." She rose and headed for the book aisles. She didn't see the librarian anywhere around.

Where would a Scottish history book be? She found an open computer, sat down, and entered her password. After typing "Scotland" in the search box, she discovered the 900-section held the European books.

That's in the back of the library.

Julie stood and stepped away from the line of computers. Dillon and Darby waved at her as they exited, following their teacher back to the classroom.

The library seemed almost empty. The new section of the library had books that went only to the 500s. Julie headed for an older section and turned down a short passageway. A sign read "600–900" with an arrow pointing to the left. She turned and entered a room.

The one window in the room had been shaded by a tall, bushy pine tree long ago. A dim fluorescent light flickered in the ceiling. Beside a wall, a collection of medieval artifacts sat on a display table—rough-edged coins, some pottery, a ring with a cross, and a wooden helmet. She lightly touched the top of the helmet. *Where did our library get these?*

She headed to the shelves and found the 800s. The books she needed were on the next aisle. Julie turned a corner.

Whop! A heavy thud behind her made her jump. She'd passed a desk and knocked a dictionary to the floor. Julie replaced the book and headed for the 900s. Just ahead, a creaking sound came from the next aisle.

"Looking for something?" Miss Duncan pushed a library cart into sight.

"Oh—I didn't know you were there." Julie laid a hand across her chest. "Yes, could you help me?"

The new librarian adjusted her glasses and waited.

"A friend of mine found a really old book. Scottish, I think?"

"Matt Silvers is your friend, lass?"

"Yeah. Do you know where it is?"

Julie realized that Miss Duncan's thick glasses made her look older. Close up, her eyelashes swept across her creamy, smooth skin. And her eyes were so blue they almost looked purple!

The dismissal tone sounded, ending her study hall. Julie flinched, but Miss Duncan seemed not in a hurry.

"Bring Matt and your other friend Ryan. You three meet me here after school." She gazed at Julie. "I'll find the book for you." Miss Duncan nodded and pushed her cart to the next aisle.

Julie didn't know if it was the artifacts, the dusty dictionary, or the way Miss Duncan had seemed all mysterious. But Julie wanted to get out of there. She headed for the library tables and retrieved her purse and bag. Maybe she could catch Matt and Ryan before they headed home.

CHAPTER FOUR

WHOOSH

Matt headed toward the school exit after the dismissal bell. On his way, Ryan caught him in the hall.

"Matt!" Ryan sounded out of breath. "Can you stay after? Julie told me the new library teacher wants to meet with us."

"Now?" Through the lobby windows, he spied students loading onto his bus. He didn't want to miss his ride, but he'd been thinking about the painting and the chest all afternoon.

"I texted my mom that I was staying after," Ryan said. "She's going to pick me up later. You can ride with us."

"Yeah, if my mother says it's okay." Matt sat on a padded bench in the lobby and texted his parents.

Julie appeared around the corner. "Matt? Glad we caught you."

Matt's watch buzzed, and he glanced at the screen. "Mom says it's okay if I ride home with you." He turned to Julie. "So, what's up with Miss Duncan? Did she find the book?"

"Not exactly." Julie fumed. "The bell rang right before she found it. The funny thing is, it's almost like she wanted the three of us together before she opened it."

"Let's check it out." Matt headed toward the library, his friends trailing behind. In front of them, the principal's office seemed deserted. The light shining through the glass wall of the office dimmed as his assistant, Miss Prentiss, switched off a row of overhead lights. Principal Harris put on his jacket.

Ahead, the polished library doors were closed, and the lights were off.

"Maybe we're too late," Julie said.

Matt peered through a glass sidelight next to the doors. The computer screens inside were dark. No after-school club met. No one had stayed to catch up on homework or for detention. He squinted to look closer. A single candle glowed from the librarian's desk.

"I don't think we're late. There's a candle on the desk," Matt said.

"Is it lit?" Julie's eyebrows rose.

Ryan peeked over Matt's shoulder. "Yeah. Hope the fire alarms don't go off."

The door suddenly opened with a loud *click*. Miss Duncan stood in the opening. "I've been waiting for you." She stood against the door lever and stepped back to push it further open. "Come in. I have something to show you."

Julie drifted inside, her arms crossed. Matt and Ryan followed.

"Why the candle?" Julie asked.

"Oh, lass. You know—a wee bit of scent after a busy day. A nice evergreen fragrance. Reminds me of the forests surrounding the glade."

"The glade?" Matt asked.

"My bonnie home, Matt Silvers."

"Is the book still in the back?" Julie asked.

"No, I've brought it up front." Miss Duncan nodded toward a long table.

Ryan hurried over to the large book. His hand swept over the embossed golden letters of the front cover. The raised title made him frown. "This is the book? But what does it say?"

"Treasure of the Highlands," Matt said as he slid beside Ryan. "I can show you the page."

"A certain page has your attention, lad?" Miss Duncan drew closer, facing them across the table.

"It's the one with the red chest," Julie blurted out as she sidled next to Matt.

"Oh, yes. The red chest. I know right where it 'tis." The librarian flipped to the illustration without rifling through the front pages.

Matt gazed at the picture and felt the warmth of the crackling fire in the fireplace. Ryan bent closer, and Julie gingerly touched the picture. His friends' eyes widened when they saw the chest in the painting. Ryan's mouth dropped open.

"A mysterious picture, that one," Miss Duncan said. "Oh, the candle! It looks very much like the one on my desk. Don't you think?"

Matt zeroed in on her desk. Sure enough, the candle looked like the one in the book.

"Yeah," Julie said. "It's almost as if the picture of the candle has become real."

A chirp sounded from a corner of the library.

"What's that?" Matt left the table and followed the chirping sound down a row of shelves to a reading area. Two soft chairs sat next to the windows. Between them, a round-top bird cage hung suspended from the ceiling on a golden chain. A dark bird sat perched inside. The smell of bird food and cedar shavings drifted out between the bars.

Ryan came up beside him. "Where did that bird come from?"

Julie joined them and peered into the cage. "Its feathers are dark, but there's purple and green underneath its wings."

Miss Duncan spoke from behind them. "Aye, and it has a yellow beak. She lifted the cage door, and the bird swept out. "I think it's time our friend Starling had a wee bit of freedom."

Starling circled the room near the ceiling, then swept to the front desk and landed beside the candle.

"Wait a minute!" Ryan said. "Wasn't there a bird like that in the picture too?" He hurried back to the table. Matt and Julie followed.

"Look, in the picture! The same bird is on the window sill!" Ryan pointed at the book, not touching it—as if it had secret powers.

"Oh, there it is!" Julie cried.

Miss Duncan stood a distance away, arms crossed, observing them.

A chill ran down Matt's back. Like an icicle. Again. "What's going on?"

Miss Duncan turned and faced the wall. When she turned back, she wore a glistening white gown. Her face glowed as bright as the sun—the dark library exploded with a burst of light, then calmed to a golden hue.

"Whoa!" Matt shouted.

Ryan and Julie backed against the library shelves.

Matt noticed two lacy wings folded behind the woman's bright apparel. "You're her, aren't you?"

"Her?" The voice had become high and delicate. Not like Miss Duncan's.

"You're the golden-winged woman. From the winding pathway in Koinopia."

"Oh—" Julie gasped as the woman unfolded her lacy wings. "You've come—*here*?" She drew close to the woman and dared to touch her silky wings. "These look like Queen Anne's Lace."

"Yes." The woman's words flowed like soothing oil. "And you may call me by that name if you like."

Matt knew "Queen Anne" must have entered the earthly dimension from the realm of Koinopia. Her presence here meant something. Had Jasper sent her to guide them?

"Aight. I'm not up for this again!" Ryan shook his head. "I'm out of here!" He turned and jogged toward the library doors.

The glowing woman raised her hand. "Wait!"

Matt didn't blame Ryan for running. Their last search for the first four rubies brought trouble. The evil Craevin had hypnotized Ryan until he wasn't himself at all.

But their visits to Koinopia had saved both Ryan and Grandpa. And just about the whole school. Not to mention his parents' computer game business.

Ryan pushed against the metal lever on the library door and popped it open.

"Please, Ryan, come back!" Queen Anne cried out. "Jasper needs you."

Ryan stopped in an instant. His shoulders sank. He turned to face her. "Jasper?"

She nodded.

He took a few steps toward her. "What's happenin'?"

Queen Anne's wings unfurled and flapped. A whooshing sound filled the library. The evergreen scent from the candle spread through the room. Loose papers that lay on the tables and atop the old card catalog fluttered into the air.

"He's been taken captive," Queen said as she rose from the floor.

Matt's eye twitched. "In Koinopia?" He couldn't imagine that the perfect kingdom had any trouble.

Queen suspended herself higher in the air. "No, he's not in Koinopia. He was kidnapped after leaving you. He's been taken to the Rim—a place of the in-between. It is not Koinopia and it is not Earth. There are dangerous creatures and perilous snares. Jasper is held in prison by the Wolvin."

"So that's why I haven't heard from him!" Matt knew there had to be a reason for the delay. His stomach turned. The last encounter he'd had with the raging Wolvin left him breathless with fright. He touched the side of his face. A Wolvin's flaming arrow had barely missed his cheek.

"My time is running out," Queen stared at the clock above the door. "Listen! Jasper and the Valenians need your help!" she gasped. "I have only a few moments." Her wings drooped and the glow of her body dimmed. "Find the Stones of Fire. Take them to Jasper—the fire of the Stones is the only thing that can free him." She turned away and wrapped her arms around herself in a protective hug. Her wings folded down and disappeared. She sank to the floor. The library darkened.

"Whoa," Matt said. He started for Queen Anne. He wanted to lift her up or help her in some way.

About then, her legs straightened, and her shoulders widened. She stood and turned toward them. The glowing gown had melted away, replaced by plain pants and a simple white sweater. The woman turned around.

"Miss Duncan?" Matt couldn't believe what he'd seen.

"It's me, lad." Miss Duncan adjusted her glasses and straightened her plaid scarf. "I had to show you my true identity, even though my Koinopian body can tolerate Earth for only a few moments. When I inhabit my Earth-covering as Miss Duncan, I am able to remain for a while. I trust Queen Anne will remain our secret."

Julie's hand covered her open mouth. "But . . . but . . ." She couldn't seem to find the right words.

"We won't tell anyone," Matt said.

"Who would believe us, anyway?" Ryan folded his arms. "What about the red chest? It's in that painting. Can you just zap it like the candle and the bird and bring it here?"

"Yeah, where do we find the *real* chest?" Matt wanted a straight answer.

"Patience, lads." Miss Duncan looked down, a troubled look on her face. She sat in one of the library's comfy chairs and exhaled, as if to expel a sad memory. "There was a great battle," she said. "When the Pellegrin left your home with the chest, they met strong enemies and were forced from their path. They fell into the 1600s, taking the chest with them."

"But how?" Matt asked.

"Surely you know . . ." Miss Duncan paused. "There are many of Koinopia who tread upon time."

"Time treaders?"

"Aye, we skip across Earth time, from one century to the next. You have experienced this somewhat yourself. When you visited Koinopia, you were outside of time."

Matt shook his head. "Yeah, but we never skipped into centuries like you have."

"It is an advanced skill." She smiled. "As a Valenian, you will learn." She paused.

"As I was saying, those of us faithful to the Eternal One were sent to rescue the Pellegrin and recover the chest. Thank goodness we found them—in Scotland, the time of King James. The Pellegrin returned to Koinopia."

"But you kept the chest in your cottage?" Julie asked. "Like in the painting?"

"Aye. Safely hid away." Miss Duncan smiled. "And I stayed in Scotland awhile and dabbled in my paints. 'Tis a beautiful land, you know."

"So where's the chest now?" Matt asked.

Miss Duncan lifted a long necklace from around her neck. A skeleton key with a wide circle at one end hung from the chain. The iron key looked as if it had been hand-forged in a fire.

"Is that some kind of antique?" Matt asked.

"'Tis very old. But it is not the key that is important, lad. It is what it can unlock." Miss Duncan moved behind her oak desk. She leaned to one side and inserted the key into the lock of the bottom desk drawer. She turned it and pulled out the creaking drawer. A smile touched her face. "Come around and see for yourself."

Matt skimmed around the desk and looked into the drawer. "The chest is here!"

Ryan and Julie joined him.

"And the four rubies are still on top," Julie said. "I'm surprised someone didn't try to steal them."

"Once, thieves did break into my home," Miss Duncan said. "The townsfolk say they were fairies. And the spirit worshippers—the Druids—ransacked my cottage and took my belongings. Starling escaped capture and guided me to a cave where my belongings were hidden." Miss Duncan smoothed the bird's feathers.

"You mean the candle?" Julie asked. "And those artifacts? The things in the old section of the library? The helmet, the coins, and the cross ring?"

"Aye. And the chest. Those things we recovered. The red chest was a bitter loss to the Druids and they still search for it.

"I kept the chest, but to my sorrow, I lost the Stones of Fire. The Stones were forged on a high mountain in Koinopia and have special power."

"So the Druids still have them?" Matt asked.

Miss Duncan nodded. "The Stones have been lost for centuries. But it is their power that will free Jasper." She faced Matt. "You must find them in Scotland."

"It's a whole different country!" Matt protested.

Ryan touched Matt's elbow. "Dude, it's a whole different continent."

Matt frowned. "There's no way I can find them."

"You will have help," Miss Duncan said. "The message of the next ruby will guide you on your quest."

"I should visit Koinopia *now*?" Matt shook his head. "But I still need the fifth ruby."

She pointed toward the book on the table. "Turn it over."

Matt scooted the heavy book toward him, placed one hand on the front and the other underneath, then flipped it over.

"Zow," Ryan said.

There, embedded in the leather of the back cover, rested another ruby.

CHAPTER FIVE

REVENGE

Matt couldn't believe his eyes. The ruby seemed to glow from within the rich leather. He reached for the ruby and glanced at Miss Duncan. When she nodded her okay, Matt grasped the gem and slipped it into the pocket of his jeans.

"I've also come to warn ya." Miss Duncan lifted a hand. Starling flew to her and perched on her outstretched finger.

"Warn us about what?" Julie asked.

"It's a who, lass. Ancient foes have arrived in Baywood—the Skinks."

"The Skinks?" Matt wrinkled his nose as if she'd said "stinks."

"The Skinks are wily creatures," Miss Duncan explained. "Always slipping in and out of places unexpected. Much like lizards, with long tongues and pointy humps down their backs. About the size of your shoe."

"Are they here?" Matt asked.

"Yes, lad."

"How did they get here?" Julie frowned.

"Ooh, lass. A particular set of circumstances must be in place. It's a curious happening—a full moon and fire upon the water. This opens the way for them, from the depths of the Dark Void."

"There was a full moon about two weeks ago," Ryan said.

"There was a lot of rain too," Julie remembered.

"A gas station flooded," Matt said. "I saw it on the news. There was an oil slick on the water and then an explosion."

"There you have it." Miss Duncan nodded. "A full moon and fire on the water. And they've come in."

"But why are they here?" Matt asked.

"To take revenge on Baywood. When you defeated the Crae-vin and the Dweller of the Dark Void, you turned them back and humiliated them." She tilted her head. "The Dweller schemes against Jasper and those who join him. The Skinks confuse and delay the Earth people who are seeking Koinopia. That is why they stir up chaos and confusion."

Matt sighed. "Are they dangerous?"

"The Skinks bring an unusual sickness. Their tails are slick, and their trails are slimy. It's the slime that causes people to feel woozy. People start to say things they don't mean. The thoughts are clear in their minds, but when they open their mouths, it comes out all wrong."

"So we've got to run off these Skinks?" Matt adjusted the strap of his bag on his shoulder.

"If you don't, they'll be stirrin' up trouble," Miss Duncan shook her head.

"So how do we get rid of them?" Julie frowned.

"Ice water and peacock feathers," Miss Duncan said, as if these things were easy to find together.

"So what do we do first?" Matt asked.

Miss Duncan turned to Matt. "Visit Koinopia first, and then you must go to Scotland."

"Are we going to Koinopia with Matt?" Julie asked.

"Matt must pass three tests," Miss Duncan said. "And his path will be different this time."

"That's a 'no,'" Ryan added. "Besides, I'm leaving for basket-ball camp during break. Don't want anything messin' that up."

Miss Duncan lifted Starling toward Julie, and she opened her hand to hold the bird. "You've a special touch with our feathered friends," Miss Duncan said. "They will guide you to the Skinks and help you send them back to the Dark Void."

"But I don't like lizards," Julie shivered. "They're cold and creepy. Plus, you never know when they're going to zip around you. Or run across your foot."

"My head is spinnin'!" Ryan said. "Matt journeys to Koinopia and receives a new message, which helps him find the Stones of Fire—in *Scotland*?" Ryan shook his head.

Miss Duncan observed Ryan. "You still have the Wonder Wafers that Jasper gave you?'"

"*Do* you?" Matt looked at his friend. He couldn't believe Ryan still had the wafers Jasper had given them when they'd vis-ited the Crystal Cavern.

Ryan looked down. "Yeah." He glanced at Matt, then Julie. "I saved one. I've kept it in my coat pocket for emergencies—in case I ever need any extra energy."

"The wafers *are* delicious," Miss Duncan said. "But they also give you great strength. A strength that can be dangerous in this world." She looked intently at Ryan. "Save the wafer for Matt. When he returns with the Stones of Fire, a taste of it will take him to the Rim."

The library lit up again, but it wasn't Queen Anne making an appearance. Ryan strode to the windows and looked out. "It's my mom."

Julie glanced at the clock. "Time sure gets away."

Matt stood and crossed his arms. "Too bad we're not in Koinopia."

"Aye." Miss Duncan agreed. "You can spend forever there and return with no Earth time wasted." She walked back to the desk and blew out the candle.

The library door swung open. Mr. Harris stood in the opening, his brow crinkled.

"Miss Duncan? You have a meeting this afternoon?" He tilted his head.

Miss Duncan smiled at the principal. "I've helped the students locate a book they're interested in." She picked up the large book.

"I see. Mrs. Davis is waiting." The principal hinted, then retreated down the hallway.

"Let's go," Ryan said. He adjusted the bag on his shoulder and headed for the door.

Matt and Julie followed.

Miss Duncan came up behind them and whispered as she flipped off the lights.

"Be brave, Julie, and watch out for the Skinks. And Ryan, take care with the wafers. Don't eat one in the Earth realm.

"Matt, there are enemies you must stand against. Your journey to find the Stones of Fire won't be easy. But after you find them, go! Rescue Jasper at the Rim!"

After arriving home, Matt thanked Mrs. Davis for the ride and exited her car. As he walked up the driveway, Wrinkles met him.

Matt rubbed his dog's back and cradled his face in greeting. "Hey, Wrinkles!" His Shar-Pei barked and pressed closer.

The small woods behind Matt's house blossomed with new green leaves and white dogwoods. The beauty reminded him of Koinopia—almost. But there was something about Koinopia that surpassed anything here.

Miss Duncan had told him to find the Stones of Fire, but how? Was it hidden in a Scottish glade or sunken in a pond somewhere?

Seeking the rubies always seemed to bring trouble. Like some invisible war pushing through to his everyday life. Would there be a battle for the Stones of Fire too?

He glanced at the garage. Before, it had been a private place to open the red chest and travel to Koinopia undetected. But did he really want to go to Koinopia now?

Wrinkles barked and squirmed away. Matt felt the white stone around his neck. Jasper needed him. He could visit Koinopia and be back before his parents even missed him. He turned to enter the garage from a side door.

Mom walked out of the door, almost bumping into him. A strand of her light-brown hair hung over her face as she carried some plastic bags. "Hi, Matt!"

Matt froze.

"Sorry, didn't mean to startle you," Mom looked him over with a half-smile.

Matt recovered. "Just didn't know you were in there." The hatch was open on the SUV. "Need some help?" He sidled past her and grabbed the last two bags.

"Thanks. Just picked up some groceries. You know Grandpa is coming."

"Yeah, I remembered."

Dad came out of the house. "Thought you might need some help." He smiled and rested a hand on Matt's shoulder.

There was no journeying to Koinopia now.

"Looks like Matt already gave you a hand," Dad said.

Dad didn't treat Matt like a little kid anymore. Ever since he'd helped his father catch a computer game thief who worked at Quantum. And Dad had been there to help when Matt was injured during the big championship game. It was then that Matt realized his father cared way more for him than the things going on at his office.

Dad had chilled. He'd worried that the theft of the Starblazers game would mean the end of his company. But now that the game was safe and a hit, Dad relaxed, knowing his family and employees would be cared for. He'd even started wearing contacts instead of his glasses.

"Got some good news today." Dad shut the back of the SUV.

"Oh, can't wait to hear," Mom said over her shoulder as she headed inside.

"Yeah, Dad." Matt tried to relax and tune in to what his parents were saying. "Does this mean we're going to the beach over spring break?"

Matt followed his mother inside, and his father came in behind them. He shut the kitchen door. "I think it will be even better than that."

Mom opened the refrigerator and set a jug of milk inside.

"That can wait," Dad said to his mother. "Here, come sit a minute." He pulled a chair out from the kitchen table.

Mom shut the refrigerator door, a curious smile crossing her face.

"You too, Matt." Dad nodded to the table.

"This must be important." Matt set the bags he'd been carrying on the counter.

Mom sat down in the chair. Matt and his father joined her at the table.

"So what's better than a beach trip?" Matt asked.

"How about a trip to Europe?" Dad grinned.

"Oh, Ben!" Mom laughed. "Really?" She covered her mouth.

"Our deal with Playtronics," Dad said. "It's finally happening!"

"Awesome!" Matt jumped up and gave Dad a high five. "You've been working on this a while!"

"Yes, you have." Mom nodded, her eyes sparkling. "You did it."

"With your help, I might add."

"A trip to Europe . . ." Mom shook her head.

"Scotland," Dad added. "Playtronics's main headquarters are located there. They're very interested in the new Starblazers game."

Whoa. Matt knew his mouth was hanging open.

"But when?" Mom asked. "There's school and work."

"So our trip is during spring break?" Matt asked.

"Yes. I double-checked with the school. Spring break and a few days before," Dad said. "Wanted to make sure we had enough time for business and vacation."

"What's all this I hear about a vacation?" A gruff voice sounded from the doorway. Grandpa had come in.

Matt met his grandfather as he stepped into the kitchen. "Grandpa, when did you get here?" He gave his grandfather a quick hug.

"Just pulled in." He stretched. "I'm enjoyin' these warmer days. Spring weather is doing wonders for my arthritis."

"Hi, Dad." Mom came over and gave her father a hug.

"How is it you get prettier every time I visit?"

She shook her head and smiled. "Come on into the living room. We've got good news." She led Grandpa to his favorite recliner. Wrinkles bounded in after them.

"I can never have enough of that," Grandpa said.

"We're going to Scotland!" Matt blurted out from behind them.

"You don't say?" Grandpa bent to rub Wrinkles's head. "Where's this mug gonna stay?"

Matt and Mom exchanged looks.

"We haven't worked out the details yet." Mom settled on the living room couch.

"I'll keep him company," Grandpa offered.

"That'd be cool," Matt said.

Matt's head was spinning. Just like that, he had a way to travel to Scotland. And Grandpa had arrived just in time to stay with Wrinkles. But before their trip, Matt had to visit Koinopia and discover the fifth message. He had to go tonight.

CHAPTER SIX

SLIZARD

The day the Skinks entered the Earth realm had been a dreary day—Slizard's favorite kind. Rain had poured into the town of Baywood, the full moon barely visible behind the dark clouds. A large pond had flooded the gas station and fuel leaked out. When a lightning strike set the pond on fire, Slizard could barely contain his excitement. The conditions had been just right—a full moon and fire burning on the flooding water!

Slizard had led his hordes into the Earth realm, swimming and crawling out of the churning water from the Dark Void. They'd slithered to the old grist mill outside of town and made it their hideout. Now they'd create some chaos.

In a flash, Slizard poked his head out from the log he'd hidden in and scurried around the surrounding area. Old rotting logs lay outside the mill. Mounds of grain dust filled the inside of the building. Grassy weeds and dewy plants flourished in the yard and next to the stream nearby—choice eats for the Skinks.

How is it that the small town of Baywood had beaten back the Craevin? Bile rose into his long throat.

Jasper and the power of the rubies . . .

Slizard's collar puffed in anger when he thought of those who'd stood in the Craevin's way—that pesky Matt Silvers and his friends.

Slizard's comrades from the Dark Void had been routed in Baywood, but the battle at the Rim had turned in the Dweller's favor. The Skinks had darted and slimed their way through the Rim, delaying the people of Earth who'd begun their journey to Koinopia. And the Wolvin had scared them away.

Slizard's open mouth pulled back in a grin, and slime dripped from his jaws. Their latest victory had been the greatest—the Guardian Jasper now wasted away in prison.

The Guardian's shackles had been meanly crafted, heavy and impossible to break. No power could release him . . . except the Stones of Fire.

But the Druids had captured the Stones of Fire and hidden them away. The Druid's altar and pillars might be in disarray, but the grove remained loyal to the Dark Void. And Matt Silvers, if he came seeking the Stones of Fire, would wish he had never heard of them.

Slizard wanted the town of Baywood. The Skinks would bring chaos and uproar here. He'd show the Dweller that the Skinks would triumph where Slag and the Craevin had failed.

And Matt Silvers, the chosen one of the Valenians, would be defeated. The scheme of discouragement toward him wouldn't end.

Slizard darted further inside the log. The Skinks had slithered into Baywood and were spreading their slime, even now. He'd call them to a meeting here at the new moon and celebrate victory.

FLYING SOLO

Matt sat on his bed and listened for voices. The silence told him his parents and Grandpa were in bed. This was his chance. The darkness in his room made the eerie glow of his digital clock seem even brighter. It was almost midnight.

He crept out of his room, cradling the red chest under his arm. He padded down the stairs and entered the kitchen. Faint moonlight gleamed through the windows onto the tiled floor. The smell of grilled hamburgers hung around the stove.

Everything seemed quiet. A perfect time to slip outside to the garage.

A sudden rasping sound made Matt jump. It came from the living room. Was it a Skink chewing its way into the house?

Matt took a step toward the living room and peeked around the corner. Grandpa slept soundly on the pull-out couch, snoring as loud as a buzz saw. Matt smiled and relaxed. *It's just Grandpa.* He tiptoed back into the kitchen.

"R-rrr!" Wrinkles lifted his head from his bed.

"Shh!" Matt entered the moonlight so Wrinkles could see him. "Hey, boy!" He bent to rub Wrinkles's head so he wouldn't get out of his bed. After a few rubs, Wrinkles closed his eyes and settled back onto his pillow.

Matt patted the pocket of his jeans to check for the ruby—still there. He moved to the kitchen door and cracked it open. The wind caught the door as he crept outside, then blew it shut behind him.

Whump!

Wind whooshed through the yard, spinning the whirlygig in the flowerbed and tossing his hair. He bent over and crept to the garage, trying to stay out of the light falling into the yard from the street lamps.

The garage looked kind of creepy at night. A light switched on in his parents' room upstairs. Had they heard the door slam? He picked up the chest and ducked inside the garage. His heart thumped as he closed the door behind him.

Matt stood still and listened. The gutters under the roof creaked with the gusting wind. Out the garage window, the upstairs light switched off.

Now was his chance.

He set the chest on Dad's workbench and reached into his pocket for the ruby. Matt blew out a deep breath. He'd never been to Koinopia alone—he'd always had Ryan and Julie with him. Suddenly, he felt homesick, and he hadn't even left yet.

Except for the wind, everything was quiet. He almost wished he could rush back into the house, slip under the covers of his bed, and forget the whole thing.

But Jasper was in trouble. Matt had to help him.

I can do this. He placed the fifth ruby on top of the chest.

The ruby flared in a burst of scarlet light, and white smoke erupted out the sides of the chest. The workbench shook. Matt caught a hammer as it fell from the wall, and smoky clouds billowed into the garage. The windows on Mom's SUV shook, and he prayed they wouldn't shatter.

He lifted the golden latch and opened the chest. The rafters parted, and the scarlet light flashed around him. A whirlwind formed and drew him up into a blinding spin.

Matt grabbed the chest and held it close as he twirled up out of his garage and into the cloud. He rose higher and higher. To his surprise, he sprouted wings and started flapping.

A brilliant blue sky—brighter and a deeper azure than he'd ever seen—exploded around him. He drifted, then began descending through a new atmosphere. Below, an aqua ocean crested and rolled in lacy caps. *The Living Waters.*

Matt dropped gracefully through the air as if he had all the time in the world—he did since this was Koinopia. Below, the shoreline skirted the water in graceful curves, and the golden beach where they'd first met Stubley came into view.

But his dolphin and walrus-like friend was nowhere around to guide him now. Matt had no idea how to navigate the deep waters leading to Jasper's cavern. And how would he swim and still hold on to the red chest? He drifted through the air, away from the beach. His course headed straight into the ocean!

He aligned his legs and feet like a diver, trying *not* to make a big splash. He stopped flapping, and the wings drew to his side.

A fountain erupted from within the turquoise sea. Matt's path perfectly aligned with the center of the gush as he descended into it. A calm settled over him and he was shielded from the water—like he was entering the peaceful eye of a hurricane.

Matt glanced down as he moved through a smooth, clear corridor. Water coursed all around him. Below, crystals formed a curved dome. Jasper's home, the Crystal Cavern, appeared below him. He'd never seen it from above. Before, Stubley had escorted them along the ocean bottom and up into Jasper's presence. But Jasper wasn't here now, so why had the chest brought him?

Rising, crystal stalagmites came into view as he entered the cavern, dropped through the center of the fountain, and splashed into a pool. He blinked and rubbed the water from his eyes.

Squawk! Squawk!

A trio of Pellegrin scattered from around him, a soft wing catching Matt's cheek. The jeweled wall surrounding the pool glowed with sapphires, emeralds, and pink diamonds.

He stood in the pool and shook off droplets of water. Remembering his wings, he lifted and flapped them, raising himself out of the pool and onto the smooth floor. A Pellegrin carried the chest away by its golden ring and flew to a marble pedestal, setting the chest there as if returning it to its rightful place.

The cavern was quiet, except for the gentle tinkling of water into the pool and the soft rustle of wings as groups of Pellegrin swooped among the descending stalactites and rested upon the sparkling formations rising from the base of the cavern.

Clear emerald light cast wavy patterns upon the glassy floor. Around him, windows gave an undersea view of the swimming creatures that passed alongside. Their changing colors, fluid shapes, and expressions were unlike anything on Earth.

Jasper's quartz table stood to his right, its jade chairs carefully set in their proper places. Matt walked over and smoothed the tabletop with his hand.

"Hello, dearie," a clear, petite voice spoke from behind him.

"Huh?" Matt turned around. No one stood behind him, but there was a fluttering to the side. A creamy-orange Butterling flitted around him. The long eyelashes and winking eyes were unmistakable. "Dresda?"

"Nice to see you." She blinked. "And you've come alone, without any help from Stubley." The tiny voice made Matt smile.

"Um, yes." He softened his tone. "I had to."

"We have been missing Jasper. He has been with you?"

"Not—" Matt stopped. He could spill the whole story but didn't want to scare or worry Dresda. She seemed so delicate. "I mean, he has been with me, but not for a while."

"I see." Dresda's smile faded. "Oh my."

A swarm of Butterlings—in yellow, orange, blue, and every creamy-colored pattern—gathered around them.

Matt ducked. "But how did you Butterlings come to this cavern? You belong on the beach. I mean, how did you get through the ocean?"

Dresda's smile returned. "The Pellegrin. We sheltered in our cocoons, and they carried us here in their beaks. Then we just— you know, burst out again." She turned around, her buzzing tail facing Matt. "Come, will you?"

She swooped across the smooth table and circled the room, as if confused about where to light. Dresda finally landed on the jade cabinet. "Something is here." Her forehead wrinkled in puzzlement. "Oh, what did Jasper say?"

"There is a message from Jasper?" Matt tried to help her focus her thinking.

"Oh yes, dearie."

Matt had received a rolled-up scroll on his first journey to the Crystal Cavern. When he'd visited here before, Jasper retrieved the scroll from this cabinet. Was there another message hidden there now?

Matt moved to the jade cabinet and opened the top drawer. Every kind of sweet delicacy—Wonder Wafers of every flavor, chocolate-covered nuts, fudgy brownies, striped candy canes, small lemon pies, donuts, and vanilla cakes. His mouth watered. But there was no fifth message. He shut the drawer.

He opened the second drawer. Gemstones filled the drawer like a pirate's treasure chest. Glistening emeralds, diamonds, sapphires, and gems the color of the sea filled the drawer. He moved the stones aside. A few gold chains and bracelets were hidden underneath, but no message.

The gleaming treasure captivated him. If this were not Koinopia... would he pocket these jewels and take them? Matt shut the drawer, cutting off the thoughts.

The last drawer remained. He opened it, and every kind of gold medal, award certificate, winner's ring, and silver plaque filled the drawer.

Matt thought about the championship trophy his basketball team had won. The trophy meant a lot, but only because he and his team had worked hard to earn it.

The awards in the drawer were awesome, but without putting in the work to win them, they had no meaning. He closed the last drawer, and it clicked.

Ding! Ding! Ding!

Bells chimed and small fireworks erupted in bursts of color. When they finally stopped, a vision of Jasper appeared above the cabinet like a reflection on the water. The edge of the vision seemed fluid, like ripples on a pond.

"I am pleased," Jasper began. His familiar voice comforted Matt, but a pang of worry followed when he remembered Jasper's capture.

"If you are seeing this, it is because I have not returned." Jasper's eyes hardened. "I have learned the Wolvin are scheming against me. They may strike at any time. If they succeed in their plots, you must not give up. I wish your training to continue."

The Valenian prince Petrus appeared within the vision. "You have passed three tests—the temptations you must avoid to continue as a Valenian. By shutting the drawers, you shut away gluttony, greed, and pride. You have my congratulations."

Jasper's face appeared once more. "You have another message of wisdom. Fulfill it in your everyday world. The Eternal One will guide you." Jasper nodded, and the vision faded. The rippling edges came together in a wavering line and then disappeared altogether.

"But where is the fifth message?" Matt asked.

Two Pellegrin swooped down, each holding a corner of a wrinkled message in their beak. Matt reached up, and they dropped it into his hands. The thick, browned paper had creases, and the words seemed to have been written using a quill:

Faith is the assurance of things hoped for, the conviction of things unseen.

Didn't faith mean that you just believed something?

But did this say that the things he hoped for already existed somewhere? Although for now, he couldn't see them?

Matt carefully folded the fifth message and placed it in his jeans pocket. His ear tickled. Dresda hovered near and whispered, "Enter the light." An emerald beam streamed through the cavern dome onto the floor.

Matt moved to the circle of light. The glow surrounded him like a spotlight from heaven, and he lifted into it, zooming to the top of the cavern and exiting through it. His speed increased, and he jetted through the depths of the living water and out into the brilliant blue sky. His wings unfolded, and he flapped wildly, ascending into billowing clouds.

A cold chill touched his arms. The clouds thinned, and the sky became less bright. His wings disappeared and he was dropping now, descending. The roof of his garage came into view and parted. He sailed through the opening and knew the big bump was coming. He landed, rolled a couple of times, and stopped next to a pool noodle.

He'd returned home, but without the red chest! Had he messed up by leaving it behind? The emerald light had launched him out of the cavern without giving him a chance to retrieve it.

He patted his pocket. He still had the message of the fifth ruby. With Jasper imprisoned at the Rim and the red chest in Koinopia, only the message remained. Would it be enough to guide him?

CHAPTER EIGHT

CAPTURED

Jasper struggled against the shackles that cut into his wrists and ankles. Anger rose within him as he remembered his capture by the Wolvin. Now his days dragged on in this cold prison. He shook with fever—a consequence of his kidnapping while in a physical body. He now knew of human suffering when sickness and pain plagued them.

His assault by the Wolvin had been carefully planned. The day after Matt's victory on the basketball court, Jasper had departed, intent on joining the battle at the Rim.

But a wailing cry soon reached his ears. The wails grew louder—it sounded like a child. He hesitated crossing through the veil to Koinopia until he could find the source of the pitiful cries. He wished to relieve the suffering of one more person on Earth before returning to Koinopia.

Jasper had followed the cries to a part of Baywood he had not seen before. He passed empty storefronts and an old car lot. He found no one needing his help, but the crying grew louder, leading him to an old grocery store.

He pulled open the entrance door. The glass on the door had cracked and splintered. He entered, and the heavy door swung and closed behind him. The aging store wasn't like Tinker's grocery, with its fresh fruit and vegetables and the healthy smoothie counter. This store smelled like spoiling cabbage and rotten eggs.

The grocery was dark, and an old fluorescent light flickered overhead. Jasper had barely walked inside before a host of Wolvin threw a net of chains over his head. They led him down a creaking wooden floor to the back of the store, where a large freezer door stood open. He had been pushed inside and realized the cold freezer space led to a descending walkway that circled down into a damp basement. Jasper struggled against the Wolvin's grasp, and they bludgeoned his head. Everything went dark. He had awakened shackled and chained to a wall.

Weeks must have passed on Earth since his capture. Jasper glanced around the chilly room, and a light flickered into his cell from a tunnel entrance. Wisps of black smoke and the smell of a burning torch floated into the room. Someone was coming. Had a rescuer arrived? Maybe a mighty warrior. One who would subdue the host of Wolvin with one flick of his blade.

His heart beat strong in his chest until he glimpsed another prisoner entering his room, also in chains, a dark hood covering his head. Two Wolvin shackled the prisoner to the wall across from him, and the hood was removed.

Jasper couldn't believe his eyes. They'd captured Petrus, the Valenian prince.

Petrus remained silent until the retreating footsteps of their captors could be heard no more. He finally spoke from the darkened wall. "Friend, we are at the Rim!"

"It is good to see you," Jasper croaked. His dry throat whispered every word. "Even here."

"How long have you been here?" Petrus's brows drew together. Anger came through his words.

"Many days," Jasper answered.

Petrus shook his head. "Help us, Eternal One."

"It will not be long, you will see. The Wolvin may detain us, but they can not defeat us."

Jasper rubbed his hand. A shackle had carved a deep ring around his wrist. "Why are you here? What has happened?"

"An attack on the Earples who wish to enter Koinopia."

"An attack upon the people of Earth is nothing new."

"It is an all-out war, wise Guardian." His hands clenched into fists.

"The rest of the Valenians?" Jasper asked.

"They are still fighting and protecting," Petrus sighed. "The Wolvin singled me out for capture."

"Because . . . you . . . are their prince." Jasper spoke slowly.

"And you are the great Guardian!" Petrus shouted. "We must escape this dungeon!"

"I've sent a message."

"Oh?"

"Matt Silvers."

Petrus smiled through busted lips. "Ah, the young one." The smile faded. "But he is new and still has much to learn."

"The way will be hard," Jasper said. "Difficult tasks are ahead of him." Jasper rested his head on the rock wall behind him and breathed deeply. "I have sent him for the Stones of Fire."

Petrus nodded. "The power that will free us." Petrus paused as if he were in deep thought. "The Wolvin are planning a bonfire.

And calling upon the Dweller of the Dark Void. The Wolvin threaten to cast us there."

Jasper felt the blood drain from his face. "It can not happen! Only they would be foolish enough to believe they can do such a thing!"

"When help is delayed, they grow bold." Petrus stared at the ceiling as if peering through the leafy canopy of a forest. "Noris and the rest of the Valenians will search for me. And let us hope Matt Silvers is up to the task."

"The Earples here at the Rim, how are they enduring?"

"The Dweller casts darkness in their path. There are swamps and delaying creatures. The Skinks wheedle and disrupt, mock and discourage." Petrus lowered his gaze to meet Jasper's. "The Wolvin stalk and threaten. They lie about the Eternal One. They say he is not good. That he is not wise."

"Pray with all your might for Matt Silvers," Jasper said. "And that those thwarted at the Rim find their way to Koinopia."

"And for us?"

"That help will come soon."

CHAPTER NINE

SECRET CHAUFFEUR

"Better get comfortable, Matt." His father tapped his shoulder as they boarded the British jet—a 747. "It's an eight-hour flight to London." Brisk air swept between the loading ramp and the plane's outside door. The smell of airline fuel drifted through the opening.

The captain and flight attendants greeted them as they entered the plane. The inside of the jet looked roomy and comfortable. There was a large center section with about ten seats, but they sat in the outside sections in a row of three. The sleek gray and blue interior and the private screens on the seat backs looked high-tech.

After they'd settled into their seats and buckled in, the jet soon whooshed down the runway and zoomed into the sky. Matt stared through the clouds as their flight ascended over the skies

55

of Nashville. He'd asked for the window seat and wasn't disappointed. Sunlight glinted off Old Hickory Lake, but the lake quickly disappeared as the jet shot into a sea of clouds and blue sky.

Matt couldn't believe that only five days ago, Miss Duncan had appeared and given him Jasper's message, along with the ruby and chest. It had all happened so quickly. He'd visited the Crystal Cavern and passed three tests, then returned home and started packing for Scotland. He'd attended school on Friday, just yesterday. Now he'd be zooming across the ocean.

Excitement tickled his stomach. They'd sightsee around London before they boarded a train to Scotland. He'd read some stuff online about the UK and wanted to see Big Ben, the huge clock in the center of the city, and the Tower of London—an ancient castle and prison.

The thousand-year-old castle was probably haunted by medieval kings and the two young princes who mysteriously disappeared. Lots of cool artifacts stood in the museum—shields and swords, helmets and breastplates—like the armor Jasper had worn. Plus, the Tower had some ancient cannons and pistols. And what was a poleaxe, anyway? Matt was glad he didn't live in those days.

He'd also seen online images of the Druids and had read a few things. They wore white tunics and sometimes feathered headdresses. They'd also carried bronze sickles to gather mistletoe from tall oak trees. The pictures showed them bearded and sometimes bald.

The jet flew so fast eastward that it got dark really fast. Matt settled in for a nap and only woke up when a steward asked if he wanted chicken or pasta for dinner. He mainly wanted water and asked if they had mac and cheese. After dinner, a steward brought three blankets, then it was back to sleep.

A scuffle overhead caused Matt to open his eyes. He squinted into the bright cabin lights.

A large man with long hair had opened the overhead bin above Matt's row. The suitcases scratched and bumped inside the bin. The strange man jerked a backpack out. It looked like Matt's gray bag. The guy zipped it open.

"Hey, that's mine!" Matt glanced at his father for help, but he was asleep.

The man didn't stop. His full mustache and beard almost covered his lips. A thin headband encircled his forehead and reddish-brown hair. He opened the bag and pushed aside Matt's socks.

"Dad, wake up!" Matt nudged Dad hard. Dad blinked.

"Sir!" A sharp voice came from the back of the plane. A crew member strode up the aisle. "We are about to land. You must be in your seat with your seatbelt fastened! You absolutely cannot open the overhead lockers!"

Dad woke up and rose from his seat. "That's my son's bag!"

A man in a dark jacket stood from the rear seats."Is there a problem?"

The bearded man hesitated, then tossed the backpack back in the bin.

"No problem." His voice came in a low growl. "Wrong bag." He returned to his seat three rows behind Matt.

"That was strange," Dad said, frowning.

"Yeah. I just have a few things—and the extra clothes Mom always makes us bring."

Mom opened one eye. "You'll be thanking me for those clothes if our luggage ever gets lost." She sighed. "Thought we'd get through this flight without any drama," Mom said sleepily.

"We land in just a few minutes," Dad said. "We'll get off before that man behind us." He glanced at Matt. "Just stay together. Playtronics has sent a car to meet us at the airport."

Mom leaned forward to glance out Matt's window. "The morning sun over London is beautiful."

"But we've got to sleep before sightseeing," Dad yawned. "It's only midnight at home. Our bodies haven't adjusted to the time change."

They landed, then claimed their bags at the baggage area. Soon, a man with a sign that said "Silvers family" approached them.

"Mr. Silvers?" he said. "Playtronics has sent me to pick you up. Our car is just outside." Matt felt relief as they settled into the car and zoomed away from Heathrow airport. He didn't see the bearded stranger again.

Matt felt even better after they'd checked into their hotel room, and he stretched out on the bed. He relaxed under the soft comforter and brought it up to his chin. Tomorrow he wanted to visit all the touristy things in London, but he'd try not to get distracted. He had to get to Scotland and find the Stones of Fire.

Queen Anne had said Jasper needed his help; he'd been imprisoned. Matt wondered if he languished in a dank dungeon, wet and dark, just like the one that had held Sir Walter Raleigh and the young princes in the Tower.

Something bothered Matt. Was the man looking for the red chest? Thank goodness it now rested safely within Jasper's cavern in Koinopia.

Maybe the man was one of the Druids who knew where the Stones of Fire had been hidden away.

Matt turned onto his side. The lighted dial of Big Ben's clock shone through the window. London would be fun and exciting tomorrow—maybe he'd even see some of the Royal Family.

But he couldn't wait to get to Scotland to find the Stones of Fire. Then he'd rescue Jasper and the Valenians.

○○○○○

Mom swept into the small living room of their London hotel suite, buttoning the cuffs on her blouse. Shower steam escaped from the bathroom behind her, diffusing the scent of mango shower wash.

"Matt, are you dressed?"

"Ready to go," Matt said.

"Don't forget the umbrella!"

"An umbrella, Mom? Really?"

"Oh, right." She sat to put on her shoes. "I forgot teenagers don't get wet when it's pouring outside."

"It's our superpower," Matt said. "Besides, my jacket has a hood."

"No worries, Matt. I've got it." Dad entered the room in his dark overcoat. He lifted a big, black umbrella from behind his back. "This would make Mary Poppins proud. Or Sherlock Holmes."

"Maybe Peppa Pig?" Matt laughed.

"Good thing this hotel thinks of everything," Mom grinned. "London is famous for rainy weather." She stepped to the window and pulled back the curtain. "Looks pretty gray out there. Too bad our one day here will be wet."

"Playtronics arranged a tour for us," Dad said. "Their car's picking us up downstairs in about ten minutes."

"Considering the weather, a car will be nice." Mom slipped on her raincoat.

"Plus, we don't have to worry about other tourists freaking out like that guy on the plane," Matt said.

Dad shook his head. "Yeah. That was bizarre. Like he was searching for something."

Dad's cell phone dinged. He checked the screen. "Looks like our car is already downstairs."

○○○○○

Matt grew anxious. He'd sat squeezed between Mom and Dad in the backseat of their touring car for about an hour. He couldn't wait to get out and do some walking.

"That's far enough." Their London guide, Mr. Finley, tapped the driver on the shoulder. The car eased over to the curb.

Mr. Finley had already pointed out many of the famous spots in London—Big Ben, Buckingham Palace, Westminster Abbey, and the Tower of London. They'd even driven over London Bridge. But instead of driving by, Matt wanted to see everything close up.

Maybe they'd have time to ride on the London Eye, a giant Ferris wheel on the Thames River. It stood about thirty stories high. He wanted to see London from up there.

Finley turned to the driver. "You can wait at the car park, Stubley. I'll call you when we're finished seeing the sights."

"Right-o," the driver answered.

What was the man's name? Matt looked closer at the driver. He held the wheel with black-gloved hands and sat straight, properly dressed in a black jacket and tie.

Matt wondered if this "Stubley" knew he had a cousin in the kingdom of Koinopia. The Koinopian cousin was a Snubble—a sea creature who looked like a cross between a walrus and a dolphin. The driver had chubby cheeks and a few whiskers on his face, so there was a family resemblance. Matt stifled a laugh.

The car doors opened, and Matt's parents slid out. Mr. Finley scooted out of the front seat and shut the door.

"Carry on, young sir," the driver urged Matt from the front seat. Stubley turned to face him. "Jasper is waiting."

Matt's eye twitched. "But…but…how do you know Jasper?"

"Come now, chap! You should not be surprised to see me. After all, Queen Anne is taking a turn in your world."

"Stubley, is it really you?"

"Aye. Remember what Jasper told you? You will not be walking alone." He shook his head. "But my time is short—so here it is: You will find the Stones of Fire near St. Andrews, in Scotland. A famous golf course is near there. And don't forget the fifth message."

"Matt? Are you getting out?" Mom bent to peek into the car. "Come on! London is waiting."

Stubley gave Matt a serious look. "And so is Jasper. Hurry your parents along." He straightened his chauffeur cap. "Time to crack on. Find the Stones of Fire!"

Matt got out of the car and shut the door.

Stubley started pulling away, but a bike darted in front of him. He laid on the car's horn. *HONK! HONK!*

No doubt about it. It was Stubley.

CHAPTER TEN

FURY

In the cool darkness of his cavern cell, Jasper turned restlessly. The chains that bound him clanked against the wall. He opened his eyes.

I wonder if it is day or night?

No sunshine lit the dark cell. His time of sleep could be at noon or midnight—he couldn't tell. He also did not know if he slept only a few hours or half a day. His troubled sleep confused him. He felt his strength draining away, but to lose his mind—he could not go there. His thinking had to stay sharp.

Smoke drifted in from the dark passageway. Jasper coughed at the tar-like odor. His cell lightened as a burning torch appeared. A Wolvin stood on hind legs, holding the torch high. He dropped a bucket of water and a metal dish of watery meal beside Jasper.

"Are you suffering in your human covering, bold Guardian?" the Wolvin snarled. He appeared to be middle-aged or older, not a young one by any means. His red coat of fur had turned white between his eyes, and shaggy tufts of hair hung from his arms and belly. "We knew you were ours as soon as you heard the cries of that youngster. The one we had locked up in the back room of that grocery store. We left the window open just enough so that you could hear," the Wolvin sneered.

"What is your name?" Jasper demanded, although his voice was not strong.

"Why should I tell you?" The Wolvin leaned his head to the side as if studying Jasper. "I am getting hungry. I would devour you, but I do not wish to release you from your present Earth-shell. Or is it skin? If it were, I suppose I could peel it off for a little snack." The Wolvin grinned, and his long fangs dripped saliva.

Jasper turned away, his anger igniting the last of his strength. He pulled his chains taunt, and the square of iron to which they were connected seemed to shift in the wall. A crumble fell to the cavern floor. Jasper hoped his captor had not noticed.

"The once fearsome Guardian of the Rubies is now captive not only in this cave but also in that human body." A spasm shook the Wolvin's belly. Was the creature laughing? It gave a high-pitched howl. "I suppose it would not hurt to give you my name. You will remember it. It is Fury!"

The creature growled his name loudly as if to make the aging Wolvin more fearsome.

"Oh, you mean like fairy?" Petrus quipped from the opposite wall. "With little wings and tinkling bells?"

Fury turned and waved the burning torch just below Petrus's chin. The hairs of his beard sizzled. Jasper could smell burning hair. Petrus grimaced and turned toward the wall, away from the flame.

"I could roast you tonight!" Fury growled. "Not one of our pack would blame me. And they might even join me in a feast." He stooped to stare into Petrus's eyes. "But we will save you for the bonfire." He lifted the torch away.

Petrus opened his mouth to protest, but Jasper shook his head, warning him not to infuriate their tormentor.

"So what happened to that youngster at the grocery store?" Jasper asked. He had not forgotten the pitiful cries.

Fury looked over his shoulder. "Lucky for the lad, a passerby heard him and told the grocer of the child's cries." The Wolvin shrugged. "He was returned to his mother."

Jasper's anger simmered. *Those who serve evil do not care who they hurt.*

Fury chortled, his shoulders shaking as he left their cell, a plume of smoke trailing behind him.

So the child had been rescued. At least there was that. Jasper bowed his head in thankfulness.

But how long could he and Petrus waste away here in the darkness? They would pray and pray hard. Matt had to find the Stones of Fire and bring them soon. Only the holy fire could break their bonds.

Chapter Eleven

WICKETY AND WAVY

Julie sat outside in the sunshine. Cool air whistled around the white gazebo in her backyard and lifted the strands of her hair. She stretched out on the gazebo swing and let it drift back and forth. Spring break couldn't have come at a better time.

During the last week of school, Wesley had kept bugging her for her history homework, and the new guy, Wyatt Sawyer, sat across from her in the library every day. They'd studied together before taking the mid-term exam in history.

She'd avoided Wes like the plague but looked forward to seeing Wyatt. He always appreciated her help in class, even though he wasn't quite as clueless as he pretended to be. Baseball practice had given him a tan, and when he looked at her through the wavy fringe above his eyebrows, she couldn't help but notice he was cute.

Besides, Matt had left for Scotland. It sounded really cool, except for the part where he'd have to look for the Stones of Fire. That could be dangerous. And scary.

And what about Miss Duncan? Every time Julie had seen her, she hadn't mentioned anything about the "big reveal" in the library. She'd just continued doing the librarian thing. It was as if Queen Anne had departed and wouldn't be back.

"Hey, Julie."

She sat up and shielded her eyes. It was Wyatt.

"Hope you don't mind that I dropped by." He looked at her and straightened his ball cap, kind of shy-like. Had her father seen him from the garage? "Um, your mom said it was okay to come back here."

She scooted over. "Yeah, sure."

He sat beside her. "So, you going anywhere during break?"

"Not this year." She scooted some more to give them more space. "Mom called it a 'staycation.'"

"Same. We're staying close to home."

"Think the team will be good?"

He screwed up one side of his face. "Not yet. It doesn't help that Coach Bryson and some of the guys are out of town," Wyatt said.

She nodded. "Yeah, Matt has left for Scotland."

Wyatt smiled. "Well yeah, but I wasn't exactly talking about Silvers."

"What do you mean?"

Wyatt looked apologetic. "He's pretty low on the roster. I mean, he's only been to one practice, and you know, he got hurt."

Julie twisted her lips. It was still a mystery why Matt had even signed up this year. She'd felt terrible when that fly ball hit him. His accident reminded her of someone—Wesley.

"I guess Wes will be hitting some homers," Julie said.

Wyatt nodded. "Yeah, dude's got some power, but, you know, he's not a great pitcher. A lot of wild throws."

She nodded. "Sounds like Wes."

Julie felt something against her back. Had Wyatt put his arm around her?

"Woo," she cried and jumped off the swing.

Wyatt looked confused. "Huh?" He glanced over at Julie's spot on the swing.

A long tail trailed over the seat before disappearing behind the slats of the swing.

"Oof!" Wyatt jumped off too.

"What was that?" Julie stared.

Wyatt bent to look under the swing. "Some kind of lizard, but it's gone." He frowned. "Maybe Wes's pet got out."

Julie felt sick. It could be Wes's pet chameleon, and that was bad enough. But it might be one of the Skinks.

"Hey Julie, look." Wes pointed at the swing. "I think it left behind a little present."

A trail of slime glistened from the back of the seat.

"Eeu," Julie looked away.

Wyatt started to investigate.

"Wait!" She stopped him. "I'll just blast it off with the water hose."

"Yeah, and wash this stuff off my hand."

"You touched it?"

"It does feel sticky," Wyatt said. His eyes glazed over. "A sticky wicket is a rickety cricket."

"What?" Julie's eyes grew wide.

Wyatt danced out of the gazebo. And started singing. "Don't break my heart, my sticky-wicky heart, just don't think you understand, blim-blam." He pumped his fists in the air and boogied side to side. Actually, he was a pretty good dancer.

Julie laughed, and Wyatt just looked at her. Then his face turned pale—kind of green. "Julie, uh, see you later." He jerked once, put his hand to his mouth, then disappeared out the side gate.

She stared at the open gate. Something had made Wyatt act crazy—then sick, she guessed. The Skinks had invaded, for sure. She'd have to find Ryan. They'd figure out what to do, and it better be soon.

◯◯◯◯◯

Ryan fled out the kitchen door into his garage. His sister, Chloe, had been bugging him again. Something about helping her deliver Scout cookies.

He tapped the button to raise the garage door. It rumbled and creaked, finally lifting to the ceiling. Warm morning light streamed into the garage. He scooped up his basketball and dribbled into the driveway. He turned to face the goal, aiming for a shot.

"Hey, Ry-an." Chloe had followed him outside. Her dark hair bounced around her head.

He took the shot and acted like he didn't hear her.

She marched down the steps of the garage, then into the sunshine."Mom wants you to help me deliver some cookies."

The ball hit hard on the backboard and bounded into the yard. "Chloe, you've got that decked-out bike with the streamers and basket. Your cookies will fit in there." Ryan shook his head and retrieved the ball.

"There's too many!" She crossed her arms. "Can't you take some to the Silvers' house on your four-wheeler?"

"Why don't you just zip it, Chloe? You know I'm headed for basketball camp this morning. I'm riding my four-wheeler to Coach Bryson's house, then he's driving all of us to camp."

Ryan shook his head. A cool wind swept up the drive. It might be spring, but the cold gust made him shiver. He trotted to the basket and made a layup, then headed into the house to get his jacket.

Chloe caught him in the kitchen. "Can't you deliver these on the way to Coach's house?"

"Forget it, Chloe." Ryan spat out.

Her mouth turned down.

Great. He'd ruined his kid sister's excitement. Part of the Circle of Three came to him—*love mercy.* Chloe could be annoying sometimes, but he *could* help her out this morning.

Ryan sighed. "How many boxes?"

"Just four." Chloe's face lit up. "Matt's Grandpa ordered two."

Ryan nodded. "Okay."

Her eyes brightened. "Here's a bonus." She handed him a peanut butter cookie from his mother's order.

Ryan took a bite. "Mmm. Not bad." He stuffed the rest of the cookie into his coat pocket. But I've got to leave."

○○○○○

Ryan fastened the Silvers's cookies onto his four-wheeler, along with his camp bag.

Mom had come outside to tell him goodbye. She got all misty-eyed because he'd be gone for a week. "I'm glad you're helping Chloe before heading to Coach's house. Here's your permission slip."

"Oh—Coach has been asking for it." Ryan put it in the pocket of his jeans and hugged his mother. He didn't like goodbyes, even though he'd be gone for just a week. He'd already told his father goodbye that morning before he left for work.

Ryan snapped on his helmet and started the four-wheeler. Mom and Chloe waved as he zoomed across the yard to the trail that led to Matt's house. The cool wind blasted his cheeks, and the new pollen made him sneeze.

Was Matt in Scotland yet? Ryan had planned to leave the cookies on the Silvers's front porch. Then he remembered. Matt's grandfather was house-sitting and staying with Wrinkles. Ryan followed the four-wheeler path to the Silvers's house. He sped across their backyard to the driveway. Sure enough, Grandpa's crusty Jeep sat parked halfway in the bushes. Ryan stopped next to the Jeep and turned off the engine.

"Hey, young fella!" a strong voice called from the side of the garage. Grandpa Harley soon came into view.

"Hey, Mr. Harley." Ryan gathered the boxes. "Just came by to deliver these."

Grandpa squinted and came closer. A smile lit his face. "Oh, I'd forgotten. I'll have those with my coffee tomorrow."

Ryan stacked all the boxes together. "I'll carry them in for you."

"Sure thing," Grandpa said. He strode to the back door and entered the kitchen. "Come on in."

Ryan got off the four-wheeler and followed him inside. Wrinkles bounded into the kitchen from the living room.

"Hey, boy!" Ryan bent to rub the folds of fur on Wrinkles's head. He set the boxes on the table.

"Yes sir, me and Wrinkles been keeping each other company," Grandpa said.

Wrinkles barked.

"He don't mind my snoring and I'm getting used to him car-rying off my socks."

"Sounds like Wrinkles," Ryan said, and laughed. "Have you heard from Matt?"

Grandpa nodded. "Checked in with me last night. Still in London, I think. Already visited that tower."

"Cool."

"Seemed awful anxious to get to Scotland." Grandpa shook his head. "A lot of superstition there. Some of it, not so safe." Was Matt's grandfather warning him about something dangerous?

Miss Duncan had said the Stones of Fire had been hidden by the Druids. Did Grandpa know about them?

"Can you stay for some hot chocolate?" Grandpa offered.

"Sorry, I've gotta go. I'm meeting Coach and the rest of the team," Ryan said. "Thanks anyway, Mr. Harley." Ryan waved as he exited out the kitchen door.

His stomach growled as he headed for his four-wheeler. He reached into his pocket for Chloe's cookie to tide him over. He pulled it out and took a big bite.

Chloe's cookie had been peanut butter. But this one was white chocolatey and zingy. His heart started pounding.

He checked his hand. He hadn't taken a bite of a peanut butter cookie, but the Wonder Wafer he'd saved! Miss Duncan had given him a warning. Eating the wafer outside of Koinopia was dangerous.

He wasn't feeling so good. Ryan ducked into Matt's garage through the side door. He didn't want Mr. Harley to see him if he got sick. He bumped into the tool bench, crumbles of wafer spilling from his hand. Ryan bounced off the wall, then tripped over the paint cans. A spasm shook one leg, then the other. Soon he hopped, then launched toward the ceiling.

What was happening? This wasn't like the first time they'd opened the red chest and been zapped to Koinopia!

He started to spin. The walls of the garage warped and buckled. They pulled apart and moved back together in a wobbly dance. A heaviness pressed upon him and changed his form. His body became a shimmering glob. He was a jiggly tangle of muscles and nerves.

He cried out, but his words whined like the whistle of a fast train. He whipped and bumped around but managed to open the garage door and get out. He spun through the yard and kicked up a whirl of dust. The dusty cloud settled more dirt on Grandpa's Jeep. Ryan circled a few times and struggled to leave a message. He finally scribbled in the dust: HELP ME!

Then everything went dark. Ryan soon found himself in a crazy, wavy world.

CHAPTER TWELVE

TELLING TALES

The light streaming through the lavender curtains into Julie's bedroom beckoned her outside. The temperature and the sunny day shouted, "Spring!"

But her vacation break hadn't gotten off to a great start so far. She lay on her bed and stared at the ceiling fan as it twirled around.

Wyatt had called to apologize for getting sick, but Julie knew it wasn't his fault. She'd searched the yard after he'd left—looking for Skinks but hoping she wouldn't find any.

If Matt were home, he'd help her. But he was an ocean away.

Miss Duncan had said this might happen. How is it that she, Julie Spencer, squeamish about everything reptile, would have to hunt those lizards down and get rid of them? Where were they even hanging out? Was there one under her bed right now?

She jumped off the bed, backed away to her closet, and got out a hanger. She used the hooked part to lift the white comforter on her bed. She knelt to look under—no Skinks there.

Tap! Tap! Tap!

"Ah!" Julie jumped.

The sound wasn't coming from under the bed but from her window.

Maybe an old woodpecker had lost its way. Or it was looking at his reflection in the window glass.

She moved to the window and raised the blind.

A strange black bird suspended itself directly in front of her, wings flapping to keep it steady. It wasn't a woodpecker. Emerald green feathers adorned its breast, and it had a bright yellow beak. She smiled. It seemed like the creature wanted to talk with her.

That's no ordinary bird. It's Starling!

She lifted the blinds to the top and opened the window. Fresh, cool air swept into the room, along with the sound of her father's lawn mower and the smell of newly-cut grass. Starling tucked his head and swooped into her room. The ceiling fan spun and whooshed. Starling struggled not to get pulled into the white blades.

"Could you turn that infernal thing off?" he rasped. The fan kept whirling, drawing him closer.

"Oh no!" Julie rushed to the mirrored light switch and stopped the fan.

Starling flapped to her dresser and landed atop the mirror, his chest heaving. He bristled and sent a small gray feather onto her jewelry box. A sound emitted from his throat—not a *caw*, but not a nice twitter either. More like a low "*ACK.*"

Julie sat on the bed across from him. So now she had a talking bird in her room. What was next? She guessed it wasn't so strange. After all, parrots talk. Really, just mimic. But still.

"*ACK.*"

"Hm?"

"You need my help," Starling croaked.

"Me?"

"No," Starling rasped. "It is your squishy cat pillow I am talking to."

Julie squinted. There was no need for his sarcasm. Then, "Are you sure you're Starling and not a mockingbird?" She smiled, then giggled.

"Okay. You have me on that one." He flew over to her bed and landed between the purple and pink pom-poms on her comforter. "Let's get to it then."

"A Skink scared off my friend today," Julie said. She turned to face Starling. He stood taller than she thought.

"I am aware."

"You were watching?"

"From the sweet gum tree."

"Why didn't you swoop down or something?" She looked over his strong wings.

"Didn't want to give away my position. Until the time is right."

"So why are you here?"

"You need my help."

"You've got that right."

"*ACK.* You've seen one Skink," Starling began. "There are at least twenty in Baywood at my last count."

"Twenty!"

"*ACK.* And they multiply every week." He flapped up to her bedpost. "By the time you're back at school, there will be hundreds," Starling squawked.

"Hundreds?"

"Is there an echo in this room? I keep hearing my words repeating back to me." Starling bristled.

"Funny." Julie crossed her arms, smirking up at him as he sat on the finial.

"Not really." Starling's eyes were unblinking. "We have to stop them before they multiply. You are only one girl."

"Just me," Julie said. "But stating the obvious doesn't seem like your style," she lobbed. "So what do we do now?" she said with a sigh.

"Run them out."

"What do you mean?"

"My brood has spotted them at the old grist mill."

"Your brood?" Julie asked.

"My peeps—as you call them."

"But no one goes to the grist mill—there's barely a road."

"*ACK*. You have to find a way," Starling rasped.

Julie grabbed her squishy cat pillow and curled onto her side. "Where are my friends when I need them?" She dropped a fist to her mattress.

Starling regarded her from his perch as if he were giving her time to figure it out.

"Matt's gone," Julie wailed. "And Ryan's leaving for basketball camp."

Starling flew down and landed beside her. "*ACK!* There is one more thing I have to tell you."

○○○○○

Julie shut her bedroom window. After Starling's visit, she had to do *something*. Starling had told her he'd been in the trees at the Silvers's house when Ryan visited Grandpa. Ryan had been zapped to the Rim!

Now, what would she do? *Won't his parents miss him?* Or did time stand still at the Rim like it did in Koinopia? Everything was getting complicated!

"Julie!" her younger sister, Millie, called from downstairs. "Your teacher is here."

Julie frowned. As far as she knew, she was doing okay in all her classes. She strode down the oak stairs to the entryway.

Millie stood beside their mother, chatting with a blonde woman in a white rain jacket. As Julie approached, the woman turned. *Miss Duncan.*

"Hello, lass."

"Miss Duncan stopped by to bring some books you ordered," Mom said. "I'll let you two visit a minute. Millie, could you help me in the kitchen?" She led Millie away.

"Hi," Julie said. She'd forgotten about the book fair. "Thanks for bringing these by."

"Spring break is a great time for readin," Miss Duncan answered with a lilt. She lowered her voice. "Can we talk outside?"

"Yeah. I've got to bring my dog in, anyway." Julie opened the front door for Miss Duncan.

Miss Duncan exited and skimmed down the porch stairs into the yard. Julie followed her outside.

"I'm glad you're here. Ryan's gone to the Rim!" Julie closed her eyes for a moment, wishing it weren't true.

"Oh yes, lass. I have heard." Miss Duncan nodded. "Starling cannot wait to tell tales."

"What do I do now?"

"I'm afreed there's nothin' you can do now but wait for Matt to return."

"But Ryan's family! Mrs. Davis will have an army out searching for him!"

"You forget, lass. Ryan had plans for basketball camp."

"So his family thinks he's at camp? That means we have a week to get him back."

"We need help from the Eternal One." Miss Duncan's eyes closed for a moment, then she opened them.

Dad and his lawnmower zoomed into the front yard, cutting their conversation short.

"But Matt won't be back for another week," Julie shouted.

"Follow Starling." Miss Duncan raised her voice over the roar. "He'll help you fight off the Skinks. And don't forget—ice water and peacock feathers!" She nodded and returned to her car.

Julie strode to the backyard to find Ginger, her golden retriever. She plopped down to sit on the grass. "Here, girl!"

Ginger trotted over, smelling of mud, and her tongue hanging out. Julie gave her dog a big hug. "Don't suppose you know where I can find a peacock?"

Chapter Thirteen

ANXIOUS ARRIVAL

Matt could barely contain his excitement as a sleek, silver bullet train pulled into King's Cross station. He and his parents would travel on this train from London to Scotland.

Streaks of red ran down the side of the train like a striped race car. Matt had never been on a super-fast train before. The only rail trips he'd taken were the tourist locomotives at Chattanooga and Dollywood.

The hum of high-powered engines vibrated around the station's platform area. Announcements flowed from loudspeakers, echoing off the glass of the arched ceiling.

Dad motioned Mom ahead as they boarded. "Go ahead. Ladies first."

"You don't have to ask me twice," Mom said. She stepped up the boarding stairs.

Matt followed behind her onto the train. They entered their cabin through a sliding glass door. On one side of the aisle, tables were surrounded by four seats. Mom sat on one side of a table, and Dad sat beside her. Matt settled across the table from them in a comfy, plush chair. A few minutes later, the train started moving.

Outside the window of the train, the sights of London zoomed by. Old brick houses with chimneys stood squeezed next to each other. Lines of smoke rose from factories. A soccer stadium and a grand castle—Alexandra Palace—came into view. Minutes later, they entered the countryside.

"Oh, look at those cute lambs!" Mom smiled as they passed green pastures and grazing sheep.

Miles down the track, Dad spotted a famous cathedral. "That's York Minster," he pointed into the misty distance. "We'll see Durham Castle next." He shook his head in amazement. "Hundreds of years old."

They crossed a blue bridge over the River Tyne. Mom soon dozed off, leaning her head against the window.

"How about a game of cards?" Matt asked Dad.

"Sure. Got a pack?"

"Uno cards. Right here in my bag." Matt retrieved the cards and dealt them out on the gray table. Dad ordered coffee from a slim man dressed in a blue vest and white shirt. The man's badge identified him as Mr. Bridges.

Thirty minutes later, Dad's coffee was gone, and Matt had won two games. He wondered if Dad was letting him win.

"Just one more game," Dad said. "I know when I'm beat." He picked up the cards and fanned them out in his hand. "Doesn't look like my luck is changing."

"'Tis luck you're looking for?" Mr. Bridges stopped next to their table. "Maybe it's Ireland you should be heading to."

"What, there's no luck in Scotland?" Dad kidded. "No wonder I'm losing."

"Oh, all kinds of luck—good and bad," Mr. Bridges said. "But also lots of mysteries." He poured more coffee into Dad's cup, and the aroma of roasted caramel steamed from his pot. "We've got our share of ghost stories and deserted castles, if that's what you're looking for."

"We've already been to the Tower of London," Matt said.

"Aye, then you learned of the young princes who lived two centuries ago. Some believe they were buried under the stairs by a jealous uncle."

"Barbaric," Dad said.

"Aye, but they're not the only bones found in these parts."

"Bones?"

"You've heard of Stonehenge, lad?"

"We learned some things at the British Museum," Dad said abruptly. It seemed like he didn't want to talk about it, but Matt was interested.

"Lots of mystery there. The Druids are said to have had ceremonies, both at Stonehenge and in Scotland."

"What kind of ceremonies?" Matt asked.

"Oh, lots of superstition. They worshipped the Earth and followed the movement of the stars. The Druids prayed to all kinds of spirits . . . and mischievous fairies. Many bones have been found at the ancient sites."

Matt swallowed. He'd read about pagan rituals. If there were bones, that wasn't a good thing.

Hadn't Miss Duncan said that fairies had stolen the chest and the other belongings from her cottage? And the Druids had joined them. She'd recovered all of her belongings except the Stones of Fire.

"But there aren't Druids around now, right?" Dad said.

"I wouldn't say they're not around." Bridges raised his brows. "There are new Druids, a few thousand who still pray at Stonehenge."

"Well, we won't be going there," Dad shook his head. "We're going to Edinburgh, then playing golf at St. Andrews."

Mom opened her eyes and tilted her head toward Dad. "*He's* golfing at St. Andrews." She patted his arm. "I intend to do some sightseeing."

"Aye, lots to be seein' in St. Andrews," Mr. Bridges nodded. "There are some beautiful kirks—I think you call them churches."

"That sounds interesting," Mom said.

Mr. Bridges looked down as if considering something. He raised his head, suddenly serious. "But don't wander too far from those old church cemeteries."

"Why not?" Matt spoke up.

"Best to let sleeping dogs lie." Bridges nodded once, tipping his cap. He moved on down the aisle.

Matt frowned.

"That means 'don't go looking for trouble.'" Mom reached over and touched Matt's hand.

Matt sat back in his seat. Out the window, a steep cliff dropped down toward the ocean. Huge waves broke against the sharp, black rocks of Scotland's shoreline, sending sprays of water into the air.

Mr. Bridges's warning might have scared Matt away if he hadn't mentioned fairies and the Druids. It just made Matt all the more curious. And Stubley had said the Stones of Fire lay hidden near Saint Andrews.

Matt knew he had to check it out. But which church had he been talking about? And where was the cemetery?

"Would you look at that?" Dad said as he exited the touring car. He stood overlooking Scotland's most famous golf course. Mom got out of the car, and Matt joined them.

The smooth, green fairway of St. Andrews Links opened before them. Slopes of grass spread across the course like incoming ocean waves. Further down, bumps and yellow gorse shrubs filled the rough terrain. Deep, round indentions looked like big domino dots. A stone bridge arched over a flowing stream.

Before them rose a building that looked like a castle, the Royal and Ancient Golf Club. The plunging waves of the North Sea crashed in the distance.

"That clubhouse has been here since the 1850s," Dad said.

The stone building stood at least three stories high with tall bay windows and a huge balcony.

"Looks as long as a football field," Matt shielded his eyes from the bright sun.

"American football is not as popular here," Dad said. "But the game of golf has been played on the Old Course for over six hundred years."

Matt couldn't wrap his head around that. It was a long time ago. But Miss Duncan had time-treaded from the 1600s. Was the course already here then?

Their driver, Bruce, parked the car and retrieved Dad's clubs from the trunk.

"A real privilege to be playing here," Bruce smiled beneath his aviator sunglasses.

"It's unreal," Dad answered. "I'm meeting our hosts from Playtronics."

"They've arranged everything," Mom added. "Even set up a tour for Matt and I while he's playing,"

"A tour, you say?" Bruce set down the clubs and straightened his leafy kaftan shirt.

"Of St. Andrews Cathedral and cemetery," Mom skimmed over her brochure.

"Ancient, and the most important cathedral of its time," Bruce added. "But be careful visitin' some of the rural cemeteries."

"Hmm?" Mom glanced up.

"Near one cemetery there is a Druid gathering place. You don't want to be visiting at night."

"Oh?"

"A lot of old hippies and the Druids hang out there," Bruce said. "Nothin' against 'em, you understand. Used to be a hippie myself. But things can get out of hand." He nodded toward Matt. "Not best for the young lad." He had Mom's attention.

"Thanks for the warning," she said and eyed Matt. "But we're not going at night."

"A good thing," Bruce said. "Where are you meeting the tour?"

"Back at the hotel." Mom nodded toward the clubhouse. "We just came here to see the course since it's world-famous."

"That it is," Bruce opened the passenger door. "Ready to go back?"

Dad stepped over to give Mom a hug. "Have a good day."

"I'll call later," Mom said.

"Maybe we'll see some ghosts," Matt fluttered his fingers. "Or creepy Druids."

Dad narrowed his eyes. "Don't joke like that." He sighed. "Now I'll be worried the whole time you're gone."

"No worries," Mom said as she got back in the car. Matt followed and settled in the back seat. "We'll see you later at the hotel."

Matt opened the closet in their hotel room and pulled out his bag. Time seemed to be running out. They'd been in Scotland for two days, enjoying tourist sites. But he hadn't figured out where to find the Stones of Fire yet.

They'd visited the ruins of St. Andrews Cathedral, and it was cool. The twin spires of the East Tower reached high into the sky. St. Rule's Tower had 150 steps to the top. He was glad they didn't try to climb it. A wall of arches stood nearby, next to a cemetery where famous people had been buried.

The cathedral was not like Baywood Community Church. After seeing the ancient remains of the cathedral, he was homesick for his simple church back home. Thinking of it made him miss Grandpa.

Matt placed his bag on the bed and unzipped it. He'd hidden the fifth message inside a small pocket. He needed to look it over. Miss Duncan had said the message would help him find the Stones of Fire.

He lifted the crinkled paper from the pocket and read the words again:

Faith is the assurance of things hoped for; the conviction of things unseen.

There were things Matt believed in, even though he couldn't see them. Like he believed in the wind blowing, even though he couldn't see it. And gravity was invisible too, but it pulled him downhill on his bike.

And Matt believed in God even though he couldn't see Him.

God had made everything. In Jesus, God lived on Earth as a man, died on a cross for the mistakes of everyone, and rose again to new life.

Matt knew he'd made a decision to believe in God at church. And his faith had increased when a couple of things had happened.

When Jasper had spoken of the Eternal One and they'd visited the Deep Melody, Matt felt a deep peace and happiness.

Then there was the Nativity scene at school. The Baby Jesus figure had dispersed the evil Craevin like water droplets on a hot skillet.

All of these things made his faith in God stronger.

Maybe he could ask for more faith in his everyday life. When he stood against evil, he needed to believe that he'd have help and guidance.

Finding the Stones of Fire would defeat the evil schemes of the Wolvin. He needed faith to believe they existed and that he would find them.

He bowed his head. "Help me to have more faith."

A knock on the door interrupted his prayer.

"Matt, are you in there?" Dad's deep voice comforted Matt.

He got up and opened the door to his bedroom. "Hey, Dad."

"I had quite a day." Dad looked exhausted—but also happy. "I saw this down at the front desk." He laid a brochure on Matt's nightstand. "Since we only have a day left here, I decided to let you pick a place to visit."

"Ben, we've only got thirty minutes before our reservation for dinner."

Mom's voice came from the living area.

Dad nodded and closed the door to Matt's room. Matt sat on the bed and glanced through the brochure. Pictures of all the tourist sites filled the pages. There were ghost tours and fishing villages, and also a mile-long beach. *That sounds fun.* He turned to the last page.

"Visit a Historic Church and Discover Druid Ruins," the headline read. A picture below it featured a church—Dunino Kirk.

Matt dropped the slick paper. His neck felt warm, and he reached for the leather necklace around his neck. His hand grasped the white stone, and it felt warm to his touch. Was the stone glowing? Maybe it was guiding him toward this church and the Druid ruins.

If Dad let Matt pick a place to visit tomorrow, he'd ask to visit Dunino.

⬡⬡⬡⬡⬡

Wind gusted in from the North Sea, chilling Matt as he and his parents browsed the limestone shops lining the streets of St. Andrews. The salty air rushed in, bringing a briny whiff of decaying fish bones.

Matt raised the hood of his sweatshirt. "Can we get some grub?"

Mom held her hair back from her face. "Sure! I'm chilled." She grasped the collar of her jacket and leaned close to Dad.

"How about Northpoint Café?" Dad asked. "The Prince and Princess of Wales met there."

"Really?" Mom's mouth dropped open. "Is it close by?

Dad nodded. "Just down the street."

They walked on until a white stone building with a red storefront appeared. They entered through the door and found a table. Brewing tea and toasted bread aromas lingered in the dining area.

Matt looked over the menu. No hamburgers, but the grilled cheese looked good. They ordered and a few minutes later, lunch arrived.

Dad lifted his ham and cheese toastie. "Matt, are you sure you want to visit a church?" He took a bite of the grilled sandwich.

"I'd like to do some more shopping," Mom said.

"Mom, we shopped all morning," Matt whined. "I just want to see this cool place. It's in the brochure Dad gave me."

How would Matt explain his interest in the Dunino church? And the secrets that lay hidden in the woods behind it?

"There's some carvings and a Celtic cross," Matt made it sound cool. "It dates back a thousand years."

"Interesting," Dad said. He turned to Mom. "Since I have my last meeting with Playtronics this afternoon, you and Matt can visit a few places together."

"Let's look at the map." Mom put on her glasses.

Matt handed her the brochure Dad had given him.

"Hmm." She twisted her lips. "There's a castle. And not far from the area you wanted to visit—Dunino?"

Matt leaned over to view the map. "Yeah, that's it."

"The castle and church are close enough to see both this afternoon," Mom said.

"Cool!" Matt relaxed in his chair.

"I'll take a taxi back to Playtronics," Dad offered. He handed Mom the keys to the rental car. "Just make sure you're back before dark. And don't forget to drive on the left side of the road!"

Matt gulped the last of his orange soda. From the pictures he'd seen of Dunino, the place could be creepy at night. Weathered gravestones, broken cherubs, and fallen crosses lay scattered around the cemetery. Behind it, a dirt path led to a wooded area.

Dad didn't have to worry. Matt wouldn't meet up with any Druids or mischievous fairies hanging out. He'd get out of there before the sun went down.

Chapter Fourteen

THE HIDDEN DEN

"It's strange driving on the left side of the road," Mom said as she viewed the road through her dark sunglasses.

Matt thought so too. Every time a car drove toward them, he cringed. "How much farther?"

"Just a few miles ahead."

They'd traveled south after lunch. Tall grass grew on both sides of the two-lane road. They passed golden farms of winter wheat. Green hedges and old rock walls lined the highway.

The sky stretched above them as wide as the ocean and just as blue. Small clouds drifted overhead like fluffy lambs grazing across the sky. Houses of weathered stone had at least two chimneys and tall windows. White-painted homes with red roofs dotted the small towns.

Mom turned off toward Stravithie Castle. They stopped for a visit, but it took longer than Matt expected. Mom loved the large castle rooms and fireplaces, but when they visited the fragrant gardens, rain clouds rolled in the distance.

It was already 3:30. Matt fidgeted. He just had to visit Dunino before it got too late. He finally coaxed Mom back into the car.

As they drove east, tall trees loomed over the highway blocking even more daylight. The rural road narrowed, and they almost missed a turn. Mom finally pulled into the parking lot of Dunino Church. A dirt road stretched beside the cemetery.

Rain misted the windshield. Mom squinted through the window. "What a beautiful church."

"Yeah," Matt said. He exited the car and waited for Mom beside a stone wall that protected the churchyard. The brick church stood tall with a fancy steeple and arched, stained-glass windows. Ivy vines grew up one side of the building and onto the roof.

Mom pulled her raincoat hood over her head. Tiny beads of water splashed on her coat. She headed toward a stained-glass portrait and peered closer. "Beautiful colors."

"Cool," Matt said. He had to admit, the windows were impressive. But the longer Mom lingered, the more nervous he felt. "Hey, can we check out the rest of the place?"

"Let's look at the old gravestones in the cemetery," Mom said.

Matt sighed and followed her.

Some of the weathered grave markers dated back to the 1800s. Matt realized the people must have lived in County Fife hundreds of years ago. Carved angels and heavy crosses had broken and fallen to the dirt. Fuzzy moss and mildew darkened the stones.

Mom circled the older graves. She caught her foot on a low headstone and tripped.

"Ow! Where did that come from?" She glanced down at a moss-mottled marker.

"Are you okay?" Matt said.

"Hurt my ankle." She hobbled to a bench nearby and sat. "Don't think I'm up for any more walking."

The rain had stopped, but dark clouds rolled in the distance.

"Let's head back to the car," Mom said.

"The carvings are back there," Matt said, gazing down the path in the opposite direction. "It's a cool den. Can I just check it out?"

"A den?"

"Um," Matt stalled. "A stone stairway cut out of the rocks leads to it. There's a stream."

Thunder rolled in the distance.

Mom frowned. "I don't think you should go back. It's getting darker. Since you don't know the area, you could get lost."

A few yards away, a touring car pulled up into a graveled area by the church. A man in a wild-print shirt got out and opened one of the back doors.

A young man ducked his blond head and turned his broad shoulders to get out of the car. An older one followed, with long silver hair and a headband circling his head. The young man was tall, but it looked like the older man was in charge.

The two men strode from the parking area and passed the graveyard. They hurried toward the den.

"There's plenty of people around if I need help," Matt reasoned. "I won't leave the path. Promise."

A young couple in hiking clothes walked behind the bench.

"How much further?" The man asked the woman at his side.

She pointed ahead. "Just a bit more."

Matt raised his eyebrows. "See, Mom. That woman said it's not far."

Mom shook her head. "I'm heading back to the car."

"I'll help you," Matt said.

Mom limped back. Matt helped her get into the car.

"Please?" He gave it one last try. "The carving of the king's footprint looks awesome."

Mom sighed. "No more than ten minutes." Her eyes widened in warning.

Matt nodded and closed the door. He tightened his hoodie against the wind and mist. Now what would he do? He had ten minutes of freedom, and he'd traveled all the way from America just for this.

I've got to find the Stones of Fire!

But where would he look? He felt they were here somewhere. He grasped the white stone around his neck as if it would lead him in the right direction. Warmth radiated into his hand. If only he were a full-fledged Valenian! The Valenian leader Petrus, or even Noris, would know where to look. Words of the fifth ruby came back to Matt.

"Faith is the assurance of things hoped for . . ."

He believed the Stones were here, even though he couldn't see them. But when and where would they be revealed?

Matt strode down the dirt path. The woods had an unnatural stillness and the trees seemed to close in around him. He drew closer to the den, and rock walls surrounded him like stacked stones. Ahead of him lay a flat area with a dark, round opening— like a puddle.

He stepped upon the flat surface and moved closer to the water. He kicked a pebble and it sank fast into the dark liquid. It wasn't a puddle at all, but the opening of a deep well. He stepped back and carefully moved around it.

Matt spied the dark stairway that led to the den below. He crept over. The narrow crevice through which the stairs descended was barely wide enough for his body to slip through. He turned sideways and started down, slipping on the first wet step and grabbing at the rock wall to find a hold. He tripped down two steps until his shoe treads finally caught and stopped him.

His heart beat wildly. If he'd fallen, he'd be in a real mess. He sidled down the remaining steps and into the den. A trickling, emerald stream flowed over rocks and fallen branches.

Ahead of him, the two men he'd seen earlier stood beside a tall block of stone—an altar?

Matt's left eye quivered. Odd things hung in the trees around him—feathers and ribbons of every color. A weird star formed of twigs hung from a low-hanging limb, twirling beside him. An apple rested between the crook of two limbs. Coins glittered from the crannies of the cratered stone walls. Shells rested on narrow ledges. Were these things some kind of offering?

Chills coursed through him. And it wasn't just because of his wet hoodie. He remembered Mr. Bridges on the train. He'd said Druid ceremonies still took place. And mentioned that bones had been found at Druid sacred sites.

Matt ducked behind a tree and watched the two men.

"When are the others coming?" The older man's gruff voice demanded.

"I saw Moon and Krish hiking the path. They've detoured into the woods, but they'll be here soon," the younger man said.

"And the trespassers?"

"They walked back to their car."

Matt inhaled to make himself skinnier. If they looked in his direction, he didn't want his stomach sticking out from behind the tree.

The older man reached into a long sack and pulled out several sticks and larger branches. The two men heaped them together in an open area. The older one lit the sticks and waved his hands above the fire as if summoning the wind.

The fire crackled and popped, then burst into flames. The younger man retrieved a pouch from his pocket and released a stream of crushed leaves into the fire. The rising smoke burned Matt's eyes, filling the den with a woody-sweet incense.

The hiking pair emerged from the woods on the other side. Long, white robes now covered their shorts and T-shirts. The woman had a wreath of flowers in her hair.

"Shall we begin?" the oldest man questioned.

"Yes, Granoch," the others nodded.

"Krish?" Granoch peered at the male hiker.

Krish brought out a tiny triangle and silver bar from under his robe. He struck the triangle and it tinged a high note.

From behind the altar stone, Granoch produced a small drum and mallet. The four formed a circle. Granoch beat the drum in a rhythm. The four chanted together, over and over.

Matt couldn't understand a word they repeated. Or even if it was a word. It was as if they were calling some dark spirit. His breathing came in hard gulps. The smoky, incensed air filled his lungs.

The woman knelt in front of the tall stone. Granoch held up a hand. The chanting stopped.

"We've had a message," the woman said.

"Yes, Moon?"

"One who stands against us is nearby," Moon said. "The Stones are in danger of capture."

"We must move them to another hiding place!" Granoch swept from behind the altar to the oak tree beside him.

He lifted a golden sickle from behind the tree and swept the sharp blade back and forth, cutting away vines and leaves. He caught a cluster of mistletoe and pulled it down carefully, as if it had magical powers. A hollow opening in the tree became visible.

Granoch turned. "Balmore, your assistance."

The young blonde man moved from the circle to Granoch's side. Granoch nodded, and Balmore started climbing. He leapt from the ground and encircled the limb with his hands, then legs, and turned his body until he could stand on the limb.

Balmore stood even with the hollow opening. He peered down at Granoch.

Another nod.

Balmore reached inside and pulled out two clear orbs. He held them high, as if they drew power from the streaming light of the sunset.

Matt's breath caught. *The Stones of Fire!*

The glittering white Stones sparked and became transparent. The glassy spheres sent currents of light in every direction. Fire broke out from inside the crystal orbs—a swirling flame shot forth, and Balmore screamed.

"The fire!" Balmore shouted and dropped the twin spheres toward the ground.

Matt rushed from behind the tree. Muscle memory kicked in, and he sprang into action. He caught the Stones on the run and stuck them in the front pocket of his hoodie. In a flash, Matt streaked away from the den, faster than he'd ever run on the basketball court.

Supernatural strength flowed through him. The same strength that had empowered him to save his friend Bailey Price from a speeding truck. Lightning quickness, Petrus had called it—a Valenian gift.

Matt ran up the slick rock stairs without slowing down. Leaves crunched behind him. His pursuers were no doubt the hikers and tree climber. Probably all in top shape—how could he outrun them? He glanced over his shoulder.

"Stop him!" Granoch ordered.

"On it!" Moon screamed and ran toward the stairs.

"I'll circle ahead!" Krish yelled. He veered into the trees.

Matt exited the slippery stairs and ran straight ahead, toward the church. Moon's steps drew closer, and heavy footfalls joined hers.

It must be Balmore. The super-muscled tree climber would catch him. Now what would he do?

Matt left the path and flew through the woods. He had no idea where he was going. He just knew he had to get away from *them*. A bad feeling spread through him. He'd promised Mom he'd *not* do the very thing he was doing.

The woods around him loomed darker and more sinister than before.

Krish shot out in front of him. "Got you now!"

Matt crashed into Krish's chest, throwing them both off-balance. Krish stumbled back and tried to grab Matt's arms, but he twisted away.

A fluid vision rippled in front of Matt, like the vision he'd seen at the Crystal Cavern. The trees and woods before him became clearer and bathed in light. A scarlet ribbon unfurled on the path ahead of him, trailing right, then left, leading him through the limbs and brush.

The vision faded, and Matt looked behind him. Krish pushed away a sturdy limb, and it sprung back, smacking him in the face.

"Blimey!" Krish shouted.

"Matt Silvers!" A familiar voice called from just ahead, then a face appeared.

"Bruce?"

The tour driver ran toward Matt, a cross medallion bouncing off his chest. He encircled Matt's arm and pointed ahead. "We've got to head that way!"

Bruce forged ahead, and Matt followed him through brushy vines and tall weeds, the man's braided locks flowing behind him like golden flames. He led Matt over a ditch and onto a gravel road. Bruce's touring car sat in the middle of the road.

"Quick," Bruce said. "Hop in!"

Matt glanced behind. Krish, then Balmore and Moon, emerged from the underbrush. They started across the ditch.

Matt scrambled into the car.

Bruce slid behind the wheel and started the engine. He slammed it into drive and stomped the gas. The engine roared, and they zoomed away from Dunino Den.

Matt let out a breath. They were safe. He patted the pocket of his hoodie. The Stones of Fire lay nestled inside. Then he remembered.

Mom sat waiting, back at the church.

Matt grabbed the armrest beside his seat as Bruce's tour car bumped over the dirt road leading back to the main highway. He glanced at Playtronic's chauffeur. Not the typical guy. Instead of a suit and tie like Stubley's, Bruce wore a wild print shirt with jeans. His long hair hung in reddish-blonde braids. A silver Celtic cross ring sparkled from his hand as he guided the car onto a paved road.

"I think we're safe now, lad," Bruce said.

"How did you find me?" Matt asked. He shuddered to think what might have happened if Bruce hadn't appeared precisely when he did.

"I saw you and your mum when I dropped off the two men." He shook his head. "Thought I recognized those men when I first picked them up. As they walked away, it came to me. Back in my hippie days, they were among the Druids."

"And still are," Matt answered.

"I saw you hiking off by yourself, lad. Knew they'd be suspicious of you." He scooted back in his seat. "We'll be back in St. Andrews in no time."

"But Mom's back at the church."

"Saints preserve us!" Bruce uttered. He slammed on the brakes. "No place to turn around here, not until the main road." He rocketed down the road until he came to an intersection.

A red sign brought him to a stop. On the left, another car sat at the intersection. Matt leaned forward and peered out the windshield.

"It's Mom!" He reached over and hit the horn on the steering wheel.

She paused but looked like she might drive through the intersection and miss them. Her face was as white as a pillowcase.

Matt jumped out of the car and waved wildly. He ran toward her car.

"Lad!" Bruce called after him.

"Mom! Stop!" Matt banged on the trunk of the car as it idled past him.

The tail lights blinked red, and the car stopped. The driver's side door cracked open, and Mom limped toward him. "Matt!"

She pulled him close, and Matt thought he'd suffocate. Relief washed over him.

"I thought I'd lost you! What happened?" she cried.

"It all happened so fast," Matt breathed out. His pulse raced in his ears.

"I saw the smoke in the woods," she said. "I tried to make it back to the graveyard, but my foot—I couldn't do it. Then I called in an emergency on my phone. The police asked me to meet them on the main road."

Bruce had come over and stood behind them. "Mrs. Silvers? Sorry for the fluster."

"We're being followed," Matt said. "Got to leave now!"

Bruce nodded. "Back in your car! Follow me out. I'll have you in St. Andrews in no time."

Mom looked puzzled but got back in the car as Matt settled across from her.

Bruce skidded as he turned onto the road in front of them. Mom buckled fast and hit the gas, zooming behind him.

"You've got some explaining to do," Mom glanced across the seat at him.

"Promise," Matt said. "As soon as we get back."

⬡ ⬡ ⬡ ⬡ ⬡

Dad stood beside the fireplace in their hotel room, his hand resting on the mantel. He looked anxious as Matt, and then Mom came through the door.

"It's dark. I got worried." Dad took in their clothing. "Where did you go?"

Matt glanced down. Mud caked the bottom of his jeans. "Dunino church." He paused. "And the den."

Mom unzipped her wet jacket and skimmed out of it. She laid it on the back of the couch and drifted into Dad's arms. "I was so scared."

"What happened?" Dad frowned. His brows drew together.

"I just wanted to see some of the carvings and rocks," Matt said.

And find the Stones of Fire.

Mom limped away from Dad, felt for the armchair behind her, and lowered into it. "Even I don't know the rest of the story," she said to Matt. "I think you need to tell both of us."

Matt's eye quivered. "I did just like I told you, Mom. I hurried to the den, and I was trying to get back as fast as I could. And then the other tourists we saw—who turned out not to be tourists but Druids—lit a fire and started chanting. I hid behind a tree."

Dad shook his head. "What about the mud?"

"They saw me," Matt started. "And didn't like me being there. So I ran."

101

"Through the woods, it looks like," Dad said.

"And I didn't know where I was going."

"So how'd you find your way?" Mom asked.

How could Matt tell them about the vision and the red ribbon that led him out? He'd keep that part to himself. Without the Valenian gifts of lightning quickness and beyond-seeing, where would he be?

"Bruce turned up." Matt looked at Dad, hoping he remembered the chauffeur they'd had at the golf course.

"Our tour driver?" Dad asked.

"He was at Dunino today. He remembered the two men. They'd been Druids in the past, and he thought they might not like it—that I was in the den," Matt said. "Turns out he was right."

"So they were chasing you, and Bruce found you and led you out of the woods," Mom said. Her eyes drifted shut.

"Yeah." Matt glanced at Dad. "We made it to his car and got out of there."

"I'm trying to decide if I still need to call the authorities," Dad said.

Mom opened her eyes. "I've called off the police." She exhaled. "Whoever the Druids were, they're gone now. Can we just leave it at that?"

"If that's what you want. We'll avoid the drama," Dad said. "Matt, are you sure you're okay?"

"Yeah." His hands shook, but being back in the safety of the hotel helped him to get a grip.

"I just want everything back to normal," Mom said. "Aren't we leaving here tomorrow?" She started picking up stray clothes from the couch.

Dad nodded. "We'll head to Inverness first thing."

Matt couldn't wait to get away, now that he'd found the Stones of Fire. He'd escaped from Dunino Den and wanted to leave the Druids far behind. But he couldn't quit until he'd rescued Jasper at the Rim.

Somehow, he knew the Druids, the Wolvin, the Skinks—and all off those aligned with the Dark Void—wouldn't quit either. Where would they turn up next?

CHAPTER FIFTEEN

THE CREEPY CONE

Julie snapped on her helmet and biked out of the driveway. Wyatt pedaled fast, just ahead of her. They wheeled out of Julie's neighborhood and headed toward the town square. Since it was spring break, Mom had given her permission to visit the Sub Shop and go for ice cream. They pedaled for a couple of blocks. Wyatt zoomed ahead at first, but then Julie flew past him.

"Hey, wait! You're getting ahead," Wyatt called from behind.

"What? You pulled out of my driveway like you were racing me!" She glanced behind. "I can't help it if you tired out too fast."

Wyatt almost hit a pothole. He stood on the pedals and huffed, finally keeping up beside her. They stopped when the sidewalk came to a road intersection. The crosswalk signal blinked red. A rumbling cement truck rolled by, leaving a trail of exhaust. Julie coughed.

Wyatt looked over. "Next time, I'll take my mom's e-bike, and you can ride on the seat behind me. I'll turn on the motor."

"But I like to work out," Julie said. "I don't mind pedaling."

"No wonder you're so fast."

The signal changed, and Julie checked traffic before crossing the street and pedaling onto the sidewalk ahead.

Wyatt caught up. "Let's head to the new ice cream shop."

"Don't you want to get a sandwich at the Sub Shop first?" She braked and slowed to a stop.

"The Creamy Cone has sandwiches too." Wyatt stopped beside her. "Let's just head there." He had a way of smiling with his eyes.

"I'm not sure where it is," Julie said.

"Just follow me." Wyatt started pedaling, and she followed. He turned a corner, away from the square. Two blocks from Main Street, an ice cream cone and a sandwich had been painted on the side of a pink building. Julie followed Wyatt as he rolled into the parking lot.

"Wow, this used to be a bookstore," Julie said.

"Yeah, my parents were lucky to find a place a couple of blocks from the square," Wyatt grinned.

"Your *parents*?"

Wyatt nodded. "This is my family's place." He slid off the bike and rolled it into a bike rack.

"And you were going to tell me this *when*?" Julie raised her brows.

"Now's cool." A smile touched his mouth, but he didn't look at her.

She laughed and imagined what it might be like to have free ice cream any time. She parked beside him and started for the entrance.

"How'd your family choose Baywood to open an ice cream place?" Julie asked.

"We had a dairy in California but we had to move," Wyatt said. "This is the perfect place for an ice cream shop. You've got long, hot summers." He strode ahead of her and opened the door. "And nice people."

Julie felt her cheeks blush. When Wyatt said that, it seemed like he was talking straight to her.

It smelled like a bakery inside. Strawberry and fruit toppings, sweet ice cream, and the scent of baking croissants tickled her nose. Counters spread across the rear of the store and down one side. The side counter had a glass case filled with round ice cream containers—every flavor she could think of. The front of the store had sandwiches. A menu sign hung on a pink and-white-striped wall behind the front counter.

"Wyatt!" A blonde woman with a ponytail and white baseball cap called from behind the ice cream counter. "I see you've brought a friend." She smiled at them but didn't make too much of a fuss. She handed an orange sherbet cone to a little girl with a bow on her head.

"Hi, Mom." Wyatt stalled. "Um, this is Julie Spencer."

Mrs. Sawyer smiled. "Nice to meet you. Wyatt has talked about you."

Wyatt's cheeks turned red.

"I hope he told you only the good stuff," Julie joked. "Nice to meet you too."

Several tables in the restaurant had already been taken, and a line of families had formed ahead of them. The bell on the entrance door chimed as another customer came in. Julie turned.

A dark bird followed the customer inside, swept into the restaurant, and circled the tables.

"Oh—!" a woman gasped. The kids at her table ducked their heads.

"What's that doing in here?" Wyatt frowned. "Hang on, I'll get a broom." He left Julie's side and retreated into a room behind the counter.

The bird circled to the ceiling. Julie peered closer. It was Starling! He sailed toward her and landed on her shoulder.

"Ahhhh!" Gasps came from the whole restaurant this time.

Starling bristled. "*ACK!*"

"Mommy!" A toddler climbed into his mother's lap and rested his head on her shoulder.

"It's just a bird," Julie looked around, trying to act like it was nothing. "I'll take it outside." She sidled out the door with Starling hanging onto her shoulder.

Once on the sidewalk, Julie stepped away from the shop. "What were you doing in there?" she scolded Starling. "You scared a little kid!"

"*ACK!* Better me scaring them than the Skinks that are in the back room."

"*What?*"

"The Skinks are chomping on lettuce and ham sandwiches." Starling flew off her shoulder. "Better go help your boyfriend!"

"He's not my boyfriend!" Julie raised her voice as he flew above her.

"*ACK,*" Starling said. "But he needs your help!"

Julie rushed to the store window and cupped her hands around her eyes as she pressed against the glass. Wyatt hadn't come back into the dining area. A scream erupted from inside and reverberated against the glass.

Julie turned toward Starling. "What do we do now?"

Starling bristled. "Hold open the door for us."

"Us?"

Starling flew to the top of the drugstore across the street. At least twenty dark, feathered creatures sat along the roofline—Starling's brood.

The ice cream shop door flew open, and a family of four ran out. "Something's going on in there!" a young woman cried.

"I'm not waiting to find out what!" the man yelled. "Could be a robbery!" He swept the youngest boy into his arms, and the woman grabbed the hand of an older girl.

Julie caught the door after they ran out and tried to return inside, but kids and families pushed past her out the door.

"I heard a crash!" one teenage girl told a friend. The other customers scrambled to the door and hurried by Julie until the shop emptied.

Starling swept by her ear. "Hold the door and let us in! We'll chase the Skinks out!"

Julie obeyed. Starling's brood flew past her, one by one, into the Creamy Cone. She followed them inside.

A cry escaped her lips. "Oh, no!"

Chairs lay scattered on the floor and tables had been pushed every which way. Starling's brood circled the ceiling like bats, then swept through the counter window into the back room.

Julie pushed a chair out of the way. She found the door Wyatt had taken earlier and stepped into the back room.

Wild havoc had broken out. Wyatt had a broom and swatted at the Skinks as they skimmed over the floor. Lettuce and salad vegetables flew everywhere. Mrs. Sawyer stood stock-still, as white as a sheet.

Skinks worked their jaws against cardboard boxes of cookies and had managed to tip over a tub of chocolate syrup. The tails of two Skinks trailed outside the open tub. The tails wiggled and curled as they slurped.

Julie panicked. Reptiles were creepy enough, but these emerged from the Dark Void. She spied an exit door. "Mrs. Sawyer!" Julie ran to her and clutched her elbow. "Quick! Let's run out there!"

Wyatt's mom nodded. "Run . . . as fast as I can . . . shazam, flim-flam, big bam!" She broke out in little laughs and started jumping up and down.

Oh no! Mrs. Sawyer has touched the slime!

Julie spied a wet dishcloth and quickly wiped off Mrs. Sawyer's hands.

"I'm not feeling so good." Wyatt's mother turned and ran toward the door, dodging Skinks on the way. She made it outside, and Julie followed, settling her on a bench.

Wyatt chased a Skink out the exit door and landed the broom on the Skink's backside. The thing slithered away through the thick grass of the back lot and ducked under a fence.

Julie left the bench and peered through a back window into the shop. Starling and his brood swooped and swept through the restaurant cawing and pecking at the Skinks. The Skinks scurried into the storage room and out the exit door. Once outside, they exploded in every direction, disappearing into the weeds and bramble behind the store.

Wyatt came over to Julie, mopping his head with a dish towel.

"Mad crazy!" Wyatt said. "What were those things?" He looked at Julie as if she could explain—like the Skinks were creatures from the nearby hills.

But the Skinks had emerged from an evil nether world, and their presence in Baywood was not natural at all.

"I think they were lizards," Julie offered, although she knew her explanation sounded weak.

"They had those humps—" Mrs. Sawyer raised a hand to her mouth as if she were sick.

"Not cool." Wyatt moved to his mother's side and put an arm around her shoulder.

"My shop! It's a mess!" Mrs. Sawyer became solemn, and her eyes became steely. "Like a war zone."

⬡⬡⬡⬡⬡

The Creamy Cone reeked of onions, wet lettuce, and melting ice cream. Julie, Wyatt, and Mrs. Sawyer stood in the dining area, looking over the mess.

"It's chaos." Mrs. Sawyer's hand gripped her forehead.

"So extra," Wyatt said.

Julie picked up a chair from the floor. "I can stay and help you. I'll call my mom and let her know what's going on."

Two hours later, she'd helped Wyatt and Mrs. Sawyer pick up, mop, fill garbage bags, and clean the glass case. Julie carefully wiped away any slime she saw, without touching it.

"I can't thank you enough for your help," Mrs. Sawyer said.

Wyatt stood next to her. "Yeah, cool. Thanks."

"Sorry all this happened," Julie said. "I better head home." She nodded and left through the front door.

Wyatt followed her to the bike rack and caught her arm. "Wait. I can come with you, you know, if you want."

"That's okay. Your mom needs you. Better stay here with her." Julie smiled and glanced at his hand on her arm.

"Cool." He released her. "See you later?"

"Maybe." She got on her bike and waved at Wyatt as she pedaled out of the parking lot.

The sunny day had settled into shadowed afternoon light. Just a few people were still out, shopping downtown.

All this trouble couldn't go on. The Skinks had ambushed the Creamy Cone first. Where would they strike next? And Starling had told her they were multiplying.

Julie knew running off the Skinks would be up to her. Ice water and peacock feathers would send them back to the Dark Void. She'd better start searching for those things.

She came to the stoplight across from the courthouse square. To her right, yellow tape surrounded the lot where the old train station stood just a few weeks ago. Weeds had taken over. A dirt pile filled in the big hole caused by the explosion.

Julie missed the old station, and thinking of it reminded her of Matt. Where was he now? There were only four days left of spring break. Would he be back in time to help her run off the Skinks?

Matt had told her that Grandpa was coming to keep Wrinkles. She'd drop by the Silvers' home and ask Mr. Harley what day Matt would be coming back.

⬡⬡⬡⬡⬡

Julie sped toward Matt's house and soon spotted Mr. Harley in the front yard. He bent to look under one of the bushes next to the front sidewalk, then stood with his hands on his hips.

He glanced over and waved when she rolled into the front circle drive, but he had a troubled look on his face.

"Hey, Mr. Harley!" Julie stopped and put down the kickstand. She swung off the bike and walked toward him.

He shook his head. "I'm in a mess."

"What's going on?"

"Wrinkles!" He sounded disgusted. "That crazy mug!"

"*Wrinkles?*"

"Can't find him anywhere."

"Oh, no!" Julie's heart flipped over. She couldn't imagine Matt coming home and discovering that Wrinkles was missing.

"Been gone a while." Grandpa settled on the front porch stairs and took off his back-packing hat. His head brimmed with sweat.

"Did he just run off?" Julie asked. Wrinkles wasn't exactly fat, but as a Shar Pei, he wasn't the fastest dog on the block.

"I let him out this morning to do his business," Grandpa said. "I came out to fill his dish, and nothing doin'," Grandpa said. "Just like that." He snapped his fingers. "He was gone."

"I'll help you look." Julie searched around the back of the house but didn't find Wrinkles. Ryan's four-wheeler sat parked in the grass next to Grandpa's Jeep. She pushed it into the bushes. Ryan's parents thought he was at camp. They'd have questions if they spotted his four-wheeler at Matt's house. Julie circled back to the front yard. Grandpa sat fanning his face with his hat.

Julie frowned. "Sorry, I didn't see him." Then, "I'll look for Wrinkles on my way home, Mr. Harley," she said.

Grandpa nodded. "Sure appreciate it."

"Don't worry. I'll have my friends searching." Julie walked to her bike and got on. "We'll find Wrinkles in no time."

She waved at Grandpa as she pedaled away. How she wished it were true.

Chapter Sixteen

THE RIM

Ryan stood on shaky feet. Darkness surrounded him, but it wasn't night—more like the minutes just before sunrise. Above him, the rustling of a thousand dry leaves. Had he landed in some kind of forest? In the distance, a thin strand of orange light lit the horizon and helped him see around. Where was the moon? He didn't know. There was a scent in the air, like smoldering wood.

Why did his muscles hurt so bad? It wasn't like being zapped to Koinopia.

Was his body adjusting to this new place—wherever he was? It felt like a foggy dream. He started walking and continued for what seemed like hours—dodging limbs, ducking to avoid swooping creatures, and stepping around dangerous snags.

His legs balked, and he tripped. Then his ankle turned. He stood once more and tried walking, then lost his balance. The path beneath him became spongy, like a rubbery playground surface.

He tested the spongy something and bounced, then started springing from one place to another. At first it was cool, but then he almost bounced into a short tree. The tree's trunk was round and wide but hadn't grown tall. Ryan could almost see over the top of the stunted tree.

"I think it is best to be careful," a voice called from the other side of a small clearing.

Ryan squinted into the mist. He heard a plop, like a fish jumping out of the water. He entered an open area, and it grew lighter.

Now, the surface he stood on became visible. It was pink and pock-marked with holes. A head squirted out of a hole in front of him. A pale creature with wide eyes and a brown, triangle nose stared at him.

"Zow!" Ryan said.

"That might not be my name." The creature slid out of the hole onto the boggy surface. He wasn't that big, and his body was like an otter's but pale and had no hair, except for its thin whiskers.

Ryan swallowed. He hoped the thing didn't have big teeth. "So . . . what *is* your name?"

"It might be Dawdle."

"Oh." The name sounded harmless, not wicked—like Blade or Spike.

Dawdle slid across the spongy surface, closer to Ryan. "I might ask who you are."

Ryan wasn't sure if Dawdle was asking a question, but he decided to answer.

"So you might." He stepped back to a safe distance. "*Are* you asking my name?"

"I would think that is true."

Sheesh, did this thing always talk in riddles?

"If it's true, then I'll tell you, dude. It's Ryan. Am I at the Rim?"

"It might be so, and that you are in the Glops. You could have just arrived from the border with the Woodlands."

"Might be, would, and could have," Ryan repeated. "Aren't you sure about anything?"

"Nothing is certain," Dawdle said. "I could believe you are an Earple."

Ryan remembered that "Earple" was the name Dresda had called them in Koinopia. He'd answer Dawdle straight. "Right. I'm one of the Earth people. And I'd like to get back there."

"What would the hurry be?" Dawdle squished back into one of his holes.

Ryan lost patience and shouted into the hole. "I don't want to stay here!"

Dawdle slurped up out of a hole behind Ryan. "You should be like the others."

Ryan turned around. "The others?"

"Earples get comfortable here." Dawdle nodded toward a tree stump. "Will you not have a seat?"

Ryan sighed. The tromp through the woods and Dawdles's wishy-washiness had worn him out. "I'm sure I will." He sidled over to the stump and sat.

Dawdle skimmed over the pink surface in front of Ryan, gathering some kind of green herb in his mouth. He sat up and spoke between chews. "Earples don't necessarily mean to end up here. At the start, they might be heading to Koinopia."

Ryan sat straighter. "There's a way to Koinopia from here?"

"That is what is said. But it could take a while to get there." Dawdle circled him. "And who wants the trouble? We have comfortable homes and prickleberries to eat here."

"Who *might* have said there is a way to Koinopia?" Ryan decided to speak Dawdle's language.

Dawdle chewed as if thinking. He stopped and said, "This one could have been very certain."

"And this one's name?" Ryan asked.

"He is a prince, I think," Dawdle said. "But in exile or something. He is fighting at the border of the Woodlands, defending Koinopia. It is said."

"There's a war?"

"There could be. Traps set for the travelers and dismal scenes along the way might be depressing for those who journey on. The Skinks scare travelers and make their lives miserable, at times." Dawdle yawned. "I would think it is safer just to stay here."

Around Ryan, squatty trees and thorny bushes served as a border for the land of the Glops. The springy soil spread out, with gouged-out holes and fleshy pink. Not exactly stellar.

Ryan held his head in his hands. *Why* had he eaten that Wonder Wafer?

He should be at basketball camp right now with his friends and Coach Bryson. He'd be seeing the mountains with blooming trees, real sunsets, and stars that came out at night. But as good as home seemed right now, Koinopia was even better than that.

"The prince's name is Peter, I think," Dawdle continued. "No, that's not quite it." He bristled. "I don't exactly remember."

"Look, Dawdle." Ryan started. "It's cool that you are very happy here. But I'm not." He tried to be clear. "Where, would you say, is this prince?"

"At the border with the Woodlands," Dawdle said. "In the direction you came from, I think."

"Oh." Ryan looked back. The horizon now glowed brighter.

"To walk toward that light might be the best way," Dawdle tilted his head as if considering it.

Ryan's eyes drifted shut. "Tell me, Dawdle, might there be a place I could chill?"

"There is a home, I think, that belongs to me. It is not cold, but you would be welcome."

Ryan opened one eye. "Where might that be?"

"It might be easy for you to follow me," Dawdle said. "Maybe it is down the next hole."

Ryan nodded at his new acquaintance. He'd follow along but wasn't excited about the invitation. Where would Dawdle be hanging out? And what would it look like? Things were getting weirder and weirder.

A spear of lightning scorched the dim sky of the Glops. Ryan hid behind a prickly bush. It was bad enough that the place was not cool to look at. Now it could even be dangerous. He needed a place to hide out.

"It would be good, I think, if you follow me," Dawdle called from beside one of the gaping holes. He slipped down into the hole.

Thunder crashed above Ryan, and a gust of wind nearly knocked him down. An acid smell, like the smoke after fireworks, burned his nostrils. He ran to where Dawdle had disappeared and peered into the opening. A long, fleshy tube stretched down away from the surface. It looked like a throat.

"Will you be coming?" Dawdle's voice echoed up the tube.

Ryan had never jumped into such a gloppy mess. *Wonder if it's like quicksand?*

Thunder rolled above him. He held his nose, held his breath, and leapt into the hole.

Blop, blop, blop.

As he dropped, the tube gurgled like water poured out of a bottle. Ryan felt the membrane stretch and open to the size of his body. He slid down the tube, and it reminded him of the water park slide—all wet and slippery—until *pop!* He emerged in a soft, orange room.

The room looked like a page from a Dr. Seuss book. It curved in heaps and rounded edges. And smelled like yogurt. Dawdle sat along a drift of orange blob.

"You will be safe now, I think," Dawdle said. A lightning strike sizzled, and a loud crackle danced around the room. Streaks along the wall, like veins in marble, conducted a surge of power and lit a small lantern on a table.

The orangey room had no corners. There were blobs of membrane around the room. Ryan guessed they were for sitting and sleeping—like zany, spongy furniture.

He chose a blob nearby and sat down. It gave in as he stretched out to lay down. His eyes felt heavy.

Across the room, Dawdle twitched his nose and seemed to be watching him. Ryan didn't exactly trust this new dude, but he was zonked. As his eyes drifted shut, he thought of home and wished with all his heart that he were back there.

Chapter Seventeen

DEEP DIVE

After the scare they'd had at Dunino, Mom wasn't sure she wanted to continue their trip through Scotland. Matt felt the same. But Dad had pleaded with them to make one last stop in Inverness and then visit the huge lake—Loch Ness, before heading back to the States. They'd boarded a tour boat for a quick trip to Urquhart Castle.

Matt peered over the edge of their white boat, gazing into the dark blue depths of Loch Ness. The small yacht cut through the crystal lake, a foamy wake curling behind them. Two white-bellied ducks twittered as they floated nearby, then dunked under the water.

Their boat captain, Mr. McDonald, had been talking about the history of Loch Ness and the supposed sightings of the giant sea monster over the years. He tipped his white cap.

"And so, the mystery of the Loch Ness monster remains to this day." McDonald winked. "You never know where 'ole Nessie might turn up."

A cold wind swept over them, bringing the smell of lichen and toads and fresh-water fish. Fog shrouded the wooded shores and the rounded mountains around them. Gray clouds moved in above the hills.

At the end of the captain's talk, Mom clapped with the other tourists seated around the boat.

Matt stared into the deep water. The displays he'd seen back at the Inverness Museum depicted weird-looking trout and creepy eels under the water.

Ahead of the boat, the lake seemed to go on forever. Any time now, Nessie could stick his plesiosaur head out of the water and rock the boat with giant waves!

The mysterious mood surrounding Scotland made it seem like all the myths could be true. Matt reached into his backpack and pulled out a bag with the souvenirs he'd found at the tourist shop.

Ryan would think the black T-shirt was cool. And the plushie green sea monster he'd bought might scare Wrinkles, but Julie would like it. He pulled the toy serpent out of the bag. The long tail reminded him of Miss Duncan's warnings about the Skinks. Long-tailed, lizard-looking creatures. Slimy things. Worry knotted Matt's stomach.

A man rose from his seat at the front of the boat and walked toward Matt. He paused in front of him.

"Found some souvenirs, have you, lad?" He took a seat across from him. A graying beard stuck out from the hood of the man's coat. A necklace of wooden beads encircled his neck and dipped in front, dangling a brass acorn.

Matt nodded but didn't answer. He replaced the souvenirs and zipped up his backpack. He didn't want the man looking too closely. He'd hidden the Stones of Fire in his bag after they'd returned from Dunino. They were nestled in a pair of socks next to his spare clothes.

The mysterious fire of the Stones had burned Balmore. But the fire had cooled to warmth when Matt caught them in his arms and ran into the Dunino woods.

"Look! I can see the castle!" An older woman pointed ahead of the boat. A gasp escaped from the crowd, and Mom stood, trying to get a better glimpse. The boat navigated the waves and drew near to the fortified ruins. Time seemed to roll backward like the waves—as if they'd time-traveled to the sixteenth century.

Urquhart Castle rested upon a rounded peninsula that jutted into the lake like a sentry guarding his post. The rocky remnant stood with a five-story tower. Part of the castle wall had survived, and lines of stone remained where the buildings had once stood. There was even a drawbridge and a moat. McDonald had said there was a prison.

"We'll be taking a wee break at the castle," McDonald said. "At hauf-eleven, we'll be headin' back to Inverness."

Dad stood at a railing at the side of the boat. Matt shouldered his backpack and moved next to his father. "Did he say hauf eleven?"

Dad turned, his hair blowing sideways in the cold wind. "Yeah, eleven-thirty. That means we'll have about a half-hour to look around." He checked his watch. "It's almost eleven now."

Mom joined them, and Dad put his arm around her. She leaned her head on Dad's shoulder for a moment, then raised it and gazed at Matt.

"I heard that man talking to you," Mom said. "What did he say?"

Matt shrugged. "Just asked about my souvenirs."

Dad stiffened. "What man?"

"At first, he was at the front of the boat. Then he came back to where I was sitting and sat across from me," Matt said.

Dad glanced over to where Matt had been sitting. No one sat there now.

"He must have gone down to the lower deck," Dad said. "Did he say anything else?"

"No. That's it." Matt didn't want to put his mother on edge again.

"I think I'm ready for a 'wee break,'" Mom said.

"Yeah, my stomach thinks it's lunchtime," Matt said, holding his belly.

Dad nodded. "I'm ready to get off too."

The tourist boat pulled ashore at the castle's base and docked at a jetty. Everyone hurried to exit. They walked up the dock, over the pebbly beach, and toward the gatehouse.

Matt remembered his Mom's hurt ankle. "Think you can make it up the hill, Mom?"

She nodded. "Yeah, but I might have to stop on the way."

Dad slowed to walk beside her.

"If you need a snack, go on up to the visitor centre." Mom tipped her head to the right.

"We'll meet you up there." Dad tucked his hands into his coat pocket. "But there's not much time. Just get a snack."

Matt jogged up the walkway and followed the signs to the restaurant.

He entered the modern cafe and scanned the menu. The buffet line wasn't long. He picked up a tray and moved down the line, choosing a cup of cheesy potato fries and a hot chocolate. After paying, he found a table and settled into his seat.

The whipped cream on top of his hot chocolate tasted sweet and creamy. The drink gave him a spurt of energy. Through the restaurant's glass windows, the castle, dark lake, and sprawling hills made him believe he'd landed in a fairy tale.

"So there you are, lad." The gray-bearded man from the boat sat across from him. Again. *What's up with him?*

"Yeah," Matt said, and looked toward the door. "My parents are coming."

"Oh? Don't see them yet." The man stared at Matt from across the table. "Too bad they might get delayed along the path."

"What do you mean?" Matt's heart kicked up a notch.

"A bonny lass is telling them the restaurant is temporarily closed and directin' them another way."

Matt's eye started twitching. He stood and pushed away from the table.

A blonde man from the next table stood and caught Matt's wrist. Matt turned. It was Balmore! Had he followed them all the way from St. Andrews? Was the man across from him a Druid too?

"Let go of me!" Matt yelled.

Gray Beard whispered under his breath."Quiet now, if you want to see your parents! Sit down!" He growled.

Matt's heart thumped in his chest. He didn't sit down but jerked against Balmore's hold.

"Now then," Gray Beard said, "How about you return what doesn't belong to ya?"

Matt didn't answer.

"You know what I mean, Yank." Gray Beard's eyes drilled into Matt's. "You've stolen from Dunino!"

Matt reached for the backpack that rested on the chair. He wouldn't let them have the Stones of Fire! He had to rescue Jasper from the Wolvin!

"Enough of this!" Balmore released Matt's wrist and shoved him away. He jerked the backpack from the chair and hurried around the tables toward the door.

"That's mine!" Matt yelled. Gray Beard tried to stop him, but Matt pushed the table into Gray Beard's chest, trapping him in his seat.

Matt sped after his bag. How would he ever catch Balmore? Out the large windows, Balmore ran across the grass with Matt's pack and headed toward the gatehouse.

Matt ran out of the restaurant, zigzagging to avoid tourists coming up the walk.

"What's going on?" Dad yelled as Matt scurried past him.

Balmore approached the path leading to the jetty. He turned toward the beach. *Oh no.* Did the Druids have a boat waiting for him? If Matt didn't catch him, they could take off and be gone in no time. The Stones of Fire would be lost!

Matt took the turn toward the jetty and hurried down the walkway. He could hear a boat powering up. As Matt's feet pounded onto the rocky beach, Balmore threw Matt's backpack onto a waiting boat and swung one leg over the side. He was getting away!

Matt ran to the end of the dock, the wooden planks rattling as he thumped across. Balmore's boat—with the hiker lady from Dunino at the wheel—careened away from the dock. Balmore stood with his arms crossed, staring at Matt as they motored away.

He couldn't lose the Stones of Fire! Matt jumped into the water toward their boat and immediately regretted it. The boat skimmed away, out of reach.

Ice water engulfed Matt, and his fingers and toes started to numb. His legs were losing their feeling.

"Remember, Yank, this lake is over 700 feet deep." Balmore laughed.

Matt became a frozen icicle, and his vision dimmed. How could he have been so stupid! He was sinking, and his legs and arms could barely move. His chin sank under the water. His nose and then forehead sank. He tried to paddle his arms and legs, but he didn't have enough strength to move them.

He went under and darkness surrounded him. The gulp of breath he'd managed to take fought to get out. Air bubbles escaped from his lips. An eel swam close, and Matt felt its slick body against his shoulder. Down he sank, into the depths of Loch Ness.

So this is how it ends? Darkness surrounded him.

Below his sinking feet, two bright red orbs appeared and got bigger. Were they eyes? Large nostrils became clear. A big bump came from underneath him, and then he sat on something solid. He touched beside him. It felt sandpaperish—like Wrinkles's nose. The snout of a humongous creature propelled him up through the cold depths!

Matt rose up through the water. Up, up, up! Back toward the surface! His head popped above the water, and he took a huge breath.

Around him, large bubbles percolated on the water's surface, and yards away, long waves formed and moved toward the shore.

"Here, lad!" Captain McDonald appeared on the dock. "Hurry! Grab this before that wave hits!" He threw Matt a flotation ring on a long rope. Did he even have enough feeling in his hands to grab it?

Matt managed to swing one arm up and encircle the ring. McDonald pulled the rope and guided Matt back to the dock. Footsteps thumped over the planks. Dad appeared next to McDonald.

"Matt!" he reached over the water and pulled Matt up. Matt's teeth started chattering. A crewman from the tourist boat rushed over with a blanket. Dad wrapped the blanket around Matt.

"Quick! Get him to the lower deck of our boat!" McDonald said. "There's a heater in the lower cabin!"

Dad carried Matt, following Captain McDonald onto the boat and to the lower quarters.

They entered a heated room, and Dad sat him on a long bench. He took off Matt's soaked shoes and socks, then from underneath the blanket, his clothes.

Dad closed his eyes. His breath came in heavy gasps. He opened his eyes. "*Who* was that man?" He shook his head. "Why did you do such a dangerous thing?"

Feeling slowly returned to Matt's body. Dad was right. He'd done a stupid, stupid thing. He could have drowned. How would he ever explain what he'd done to his parents?

Matt curled onto his side. He didn't have an answer for Dad. And he'd lost the Stones of Fire!

What kind of son was he? He'd failed as a Valenian. What hope was there for Jasper now?

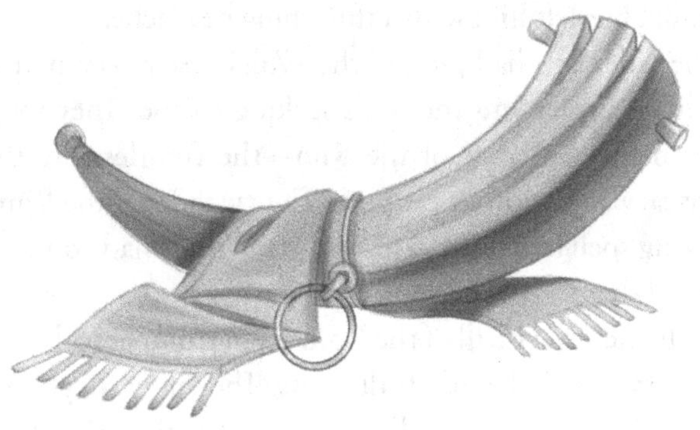

CHAPTER EIGHTEEN

THE VALENIANS

Noris lifted his head from the mound of hay he'd rested upon the night before. Sleep had been fitful among the Valenian warriors.

His eyes burned as he opened them. Smoke rose in the distance. He sat up and felt his arm. A fiery arrow from the Wolvin had grazed him and burned a hole in his fur mantle. The shaft of the blazing arrow had branded his shoulder with a long, nasty burn.

And his companions had fared no better. Strikes to the forehead, elbows, and knees had left throbbing wounds. Their hands had been trampled by Wolvin hooves and lay bruised and swollen at their sides.

Noris reached for his horned helmet and placed it on his head. Pain raged through his skull—the axe blow had not pierced his helmet but left him with a throbbing headache.

The Valenians had pushed the Wolvin back—away from the struggling Earples and the souls seeking escape. They longed to flee from the sameness of the Rim—the colorless life that left them weary and without purpose. They wandered the Rim as if a paralyzing spell had been cast. And the Skinks had confused and perplexed them.

Only the silvery trill of the Koinopian trumpet had awakened the seekers and broken their dullness. They now sought a better country. The Valenians would open a path to the Prism Bridge so that they could find their way.

"Noris?" Juman stood beside him. "A little help is needed, aye?" He adjusted his leather cape and held out a muscled arm. "A hand up?"

Noris glanced up at the young Valenian standing nearby. Juman had fought many battles, but his knees still stood strong.

Unlike mine.

Noris knew his heavy bulk made him intimidating on the battlefield but not so light on his feet. He grasped Juman's wide hand and pushed up from the hay with all his might. Pain ran up his lower back.

"You are steady, then?" Juman asked.

Noris growled. "As steady as a mountain." He held his back and hoped Juman had not noticed his wince.

Voices murmured around their camp as the other Valenians awakened. Men arose, tossing fur coverings and capes aside. Brenan had built a small fire. A copper pot swung above the crackling flames.

Ah, good. They would soon have mulled cider, a toasted crust with slathered butter, and a side of smoked meat. Sustenance they'd packed from the rich meadows of the Woodlands.

"Be gone, ye bad omen!" Brenan yelled. He'd reached into the long sack he'd kept for bread crusts, but instead of bread, pulled out a long tail. A Skink dangled from his hand. He tossed the creature into the fire. "Back to where ye came from, ye slimy one!" The Skink landed in the coals but soon burrowed into the damp earth beneath the fire.

"Must we always be on our guard!" Noris complained. The Skinks were a nuisance, not as mighty as the Wolvin, but a pestilence to be sure.

Brenan found another sack of bread and provisions. Soon, the whole camp had relished a meal.

Noris waited until all had eaten. They would be thinkin' more clearly. He would lay out the way forward. They must quench the fires threatening the Woodlands and rescue Petrus from prison. Time, as it passed here at the Rim, was not their friend.

Noris reached into his pack. A red scarf enfolded the hunting horn he'd hidden inside. He removed the scarf and raised the instrument to his lips, blowing a soft, vibrating tone. The men's talk quieted, and they moved toward him with surprised expressions.

"Petrus's horn?" A tall Valenian came near, a smile spreading across his face.

"Here, here!" The men repeated as they gathered in a circle around.

"That be truth," Noris nodded. "Most honored Petrus, clever prince that he is, managed to hide away his horn and scarf in my pack."

"It is help sent from the Eternal One," Juman said.

Noris lowered his eyes."Let us hope. And that he will send more."

"What of the young one, Matt Silvers?" Juman asked.

"Jasper is in charge with young Silvers," Noris answered. "The chest and rubies have guided his way to Koinopia, but the path to the Rim he has yet to journey." A stab of worry hit Noris. Surely, Jasper knew of their distress. Where was he?

"Aye!" the men shouted.

Noris looked upon each one. "We must put out the fires lurking close to the Woodlands." He fisted his hand. "The stink of smoke threatens the lives of our Woodland friends. The beauty of our forest home is scarred by the darkness spreading from the Rim!"

"For Petrus and the Woodlands!" a voice shouted.

"What is our next move?" Juman asked.

"Find our way through this smoke. And to the prison that holds our leader."

"Where have they taken him?" Juman asked.

"Not far from here is Bounded Hollow," Noris said. "An old prison."

"Not Bounded Hollow!" An older Valenian pushed forward through the crowd. A patch of gray hair sat atop his balding head. Although not as strong as the younger ones, Adren had a keen eye with bow and arrow.

"I have been imprisoned in that cave! The Wolvin there are more vicious than the rest. And seek to devour!" Adren rubbed an angry scar beneath his chin. "I cannot forget my time there. They have a bonfire every full moon. And empty the prison of their captives."

The tribe erupted in shouts. "It can not be!"

"Our leader has been prisoner two weeks," Noris said.

"Then we don't have much time," Juman said.

"Such as it is," Adren huffed. "Time at the Rim is unpredictable. It seems to flee quickly when you need more of it. And stretches out, not to be endured, when you wish it to pass."

Jasper glanced across the prison chamber. The hollows under Petrus's eyes had grown deeper. His muscles protruded upon skinny arms and legs.

"Not to worry, Petrus," Jasper breathed. "Help is coming."

"They gather limbs and cut the trees of the Woodlands. I have heard the chop of the axe above us. They are preparing a pyre," Petrus answered weakly.

"Not for us!" Jasper exclaimed.

"They cannot kill us," Petrus said. "But our bodies will feel the pain!"

"No! No one decides the end of our journey but the Eternal One!" Jasper shouted. "No evil plan, no fire, no flooding waters . . . I know in my being. His plan for us is not complete yet! Petrus, join me in believing prayer!"

Jasper bowed his head wearily. Something within urged a desperate prayer for Matt Silvers. He must bring the Stones of Fire with haste! The young one must succeed!

From his deepest being, Jasper prayed.

Chapter Nineteen

DAWDLE

THURRP!

Ryan opened one eye, then closed it again.

So it hadn't been a bad dream. He'd awakened at the Rim. In the Glops. Inside Dawdle's home. But calling it home was a stretch. More like a pink, squishy stomach he'd dropped into.

"I think it is time to wake up!" Dawdle's cheeriness didn't make Ryan feel better.

Ryan sat up. "I heard a burping sound."

"It would probably be the wind that you heard. Whistling across the opening. I believe you'll remember. You dropped down a long tube—"

"Yeah, I remember," Ryan said. "But I wish I could forget."

"I think it is the week to gather our prickleberries. Won't you be coming along?"

Ryan's stomach growled. "Prickleberries?"

"Oh yes. I could believe you will like them."

"Why would you believe that?"

"What is it that Earples say?" Dawdle's tail whopped behind him, and a small wave rumpled across the spongy floor of the burrow. "Satisfying? Yes, I believe that is the word." Dawdle glided over and searched Ryan's face. "Sleep has done you good, I think."

Ryan drew back from Dawdle's pale whiskers. "What day is it anyway?"

"I wouldn't know. But you've slept for almost a week. Five days, I think."

"Five days!"

"Yes. I believe you are concerned?"

Ryan closed his eyes. What was happening back home? Coach and the rest of the team would soon get back from camp. And Ryan would turn up missing. His family would be in a panic.

He had to find a way back home. Dawdle had said a prince in the Woodlands knew the way to Koinopia. If Ryan could get back to Koinopia, Matt might find him.

But here in the Glops? Man! Would anyone ever know what happened to him?

Ryan rolled off the gloppy bed and pushed against the spongy floor to stand up.

He tilted to the right and finally gained his balance. His legs and arms felt weak. How would he even make it back to the Woodlands?

"Say, Dawdle. Those prickleberries, they give strength too?"

"A certain amount, but strength is not needed here." He whopped his tail. "We mostly just drift and glide."

Ryan nodded. He wanted to do more than just drift around. Maybe the prickleberries would help. "Aight. How do we get back on top?"

"It would help, I think, if you watch me." Dawdle moved to the fleshy tube and stood just below the opening. "It may be a few moments, I think."

Seconds passed. Ryan frowned. Maybe the tube wasn't working.

THHURRP!

A big burp pulled Dawdle out of sight up to the spongy surface. Now, it was Ryan's turn. He hesitated.

"It is best, I think, if you come up!" Dawdle's muffled voice vibrated down the opening.

Ryan shook his head. He didn't want to go through there. But he *had* to. He moved to a spot just below the fleshy tube. "Zap me outta here!"

Seconds passed. Then the big burp. Ryan's curly hair felt pulled at the roots, and his forehead, neck, and whole body stretched.

"Ow!" Ryan yelled.

Plop! He ejected out of the tube and onto the surface above.

Ryan rolled a couple of times and landed next to one of the stubbly trees. At least he was out of the pink stomach. And no lightning zapped around him. He'd find some of those prickleberries and get out of here.

⬡⬡⬡⬡⬡

Julie's watch alarm buzzed, and she opened her eyes. Morning light poured through the window. It was already Friday. Spring break was going by fast!

She'd decided to get up early to help Grandpa search for Wrinkles. After getting dressed, she stopped in the kitchen for breakfast. Mom and Millie sat together at the table.

"You're up early," Mom said, then sipped her coffee.

Julie sat with them and poured milk into a bowl of raisin cereal. "Wrinkles is missing."

"Oh, no." Mom shook her head. "Matt will be so upset if he's not found."

"Not Wrinkles!" Millie joined in.

"Afraid so," Julie said. "Mom, I told Mr. Harley I'd help him look around the neighborhood. Mind if I search on my bike for a while?"

"Sure," Mom said. "Just don't bike too far. And check in."

"I will."

Julie gulped down the cereal and hurried outside to her bike. She hopped on and pedaled up and down the neighborhood streets. That crazy dog had to be close by. Wrinkles never strayed far from home. Where could he be?

She searched between the houses and into backyards. Julie stopped and asked her friends to keep an eye out, especially those with dogs. Wrinkles might come for a visit.

After an hour, she turned toward home. She wheeled into her garage and parked the bike.

Mom came around the corner. "Julie, I started to get worried. It's been a couple of hours."

"Sorry, Mom." She crossed her arms. "I don't guess you've seen Wrinkles around here today?"

"No, we've been setting out impatiens in the flowerbed," Mom said. Millie came to stand beside her.

"Wrinkles didn't come around, but I've seen a couple of lizards!" Millie squealed.

"Maybe they're armadillos," Mom said. "They've rooted around and nearly ruined my flower beds."

Julie thought she'd be sick. They weren't armadillos. The Skinks were invading her Mom's garden!

Julie looked around for slime but didn't see any. "Uh, Mom. Don't get around those lizards. They just invaded the Creamy Cone. They're nasty."

"I won't. You can be sure of that." Mom touched Millie's shoulder. "Come on. Let's go inside." She turned to Julie. "Sorry about Wrinkles."

"What am I going to tell Matt?"

Mom took off her gardening gloves. "I'll go inside and call some friends. Maybe someone has seen him."

"Thought I'd check around downtown first," Julie said.

Mom shook her head. "I don't want you going there alone," Mom said. "Why don't you wait for your father? He can take you to look around."

Julie nodded. But the town square wasn't the only place she knew she had to go.

Starling had told her the Skinks were hiding out at the old grist mill.

The Creamy Cone had dry ice, the kind that kept ice cream solid in the dairy case. That would help turn the Skinks back. But where would she find peacock feathers?

She had to think. And *do* something. The invasion was getting out of control.

Chapter Twenty

THE LOST ONE

Ding! Ding!

Matt awoke to an announcement coming through the speakers of the airplane.

"We are approaching the Nashville airport . . ." The steward's voice instructed them to prepare for landing. Matt buckled his seatbelt.

Was it his imagination, or had the ride back home been faster than their trip to the UK?

Orange and yellow beams of the sunset streaked through the small window next to his seat. He glanced outside. Old Hickory Lake glinted like diamonds below him. The plane descended, and soon, they were on the ground.

○○○○○

"Blasted traffic!" Grandpa shook his head. "Sorry I was late to pick you up from the airport." Grandpa eased their SUV onto the interstate.

"I'm just glad you figured out where to find us," Dad said from across the front seat.

At least Grandpa hadn't picked them up in *his* Jeep. Matt sighed and relaxed against the cushioned headrest.

Mom sat in the back seat across from Matt. "Guess you'll be glad to see your friends. Don't you have baseball practice this week?"

"Yeah," Matt answered, but didn't really feel like talking. Baseball wasn't exactly his thing. He'd joined to help Coach out.

If only he'd been able to help Jasper. He'd failed at the one thing he'd been entrusted to do. He'd returned without the Stones of Fire. How could he face the Valenians?

Stand against those who serve evil.

That was the mission he'd been given. He'd stood all right and fallen—just like he'd fallen through the deep waters of Loch Ness. Would the Stones of Fire be lost forever?

At least Wrinkles would be home to greet him. He'd missed his best dog and wondered if he'd gotten into any trouble.

"Hey, Grandpa. How's Wrinkles doing?" Matt asked from the back seat.

Grandpa nodded. "You'll see him soon enough." Then, "Can't talk while I'm trying to watch the road, son."

Thirty minutes later, they pulled into their driveway at home.

Matt popped out of the SUV and ran to the house. He waited for Dad to unlock the door, then rushed into the kitchen.

"Wrinkles! Hey, Wrinkles!" Matt hollered. "Here, boy!"

The stillness of the house seemed unnatural. He could hear the refrigerator humming. No padding steps hurried toward him.

Grandpa's hand came to rest on his shoulder. "I'm sorry, son."

"What?" Confusion unsettled Matt. Then his heart started racing. "Did something happen to Wrinkles?"

Grandpa's eyes held an apology.

Dad and Mom had come into the kitchen behind Matt. He turned and searched their faces. They looked as alarmed as Matt felt.

Mom drew near. "What's happened?"

"I haven't seen Wrinkles since yesterday morning," Grandpa said. Worry shadowed his face. "I went outside to fill his dish and he followed me out." He shook his head. "He disappeared before I could turn around."

"Oh, no." Mom sat in a kitchen chair.

Dad crossed his arms. "It hasn't been that long. We can find him."

Grandpa nodded. "Julie and her friends have been looking. Her family's helpin' out."

Matt thought he'd throw up. "I thought you said I'd see him?"

"I still believe that, son." Grandpa nodded.

Matt ran upstairs into his room. He slammed the bedroom door.

Footsteps came up the stairs, then a knock on the door. "Matt?" Mom's muffled voice drifted in through the hall.

"I'm okay!" Matt choked out. He fell onto his bed.

"We'll be downstairs." Mom's voice cracked. "When you're ready to talk, we can figure this out." Matt heard her descend the stairs.

He sat up and scanned his room. Everything was just as he'd left it. His ball cap hung from a bedpost. The picture of his basketball team sat on the nightstand. The bed was lumpy, just like he'd made it up. His spiral notebooks sat piled on his desk. Everything looked the same.

Yet nothing would be the same without Wrinkles.

How many times had Wrinkles nudged the door open with his nose and attempted to jump on Matt's bed? He didn't always make it, and Matt would help him the rest of the way.

Matt flipped onto his back. The phone next to his bed rang. And rang again.

He reached over and answered it.

"Matt?" It was Julie.

"Yeah."

"Grandpa told you about Wrinkles?"

"Uh-huh."

"Sorry. But . . . we can find him."

Matt coughed. "I'm not sure about that." His eye twitched.

"Did you find the . . ."

"I can't talk right now," Matt croaked. He'd hang up before Julie asked about the Stones of Fire.

"Is it okay if I come over tomorrow?" Julie asked.

"Maybe. I guess."

"Okay," she breathed out. "Bye, Matt."

"Later."

He hung up the phone.

He hadn't meant to sound rude. But he just couldn't talk.

Matt turned on his side, and his eyes drifted closed. Maybe he'd wake up in the morning and see that Wrinkles had found his way home. Tomorrow would be different.

◇◇◇◇◇

Grandpa shook Matt's shoulder. "Son, it's time to get up."

"I don't have to go to school today," Matt answered. He turned away from Grandpa and pulled the comforter over his shoulder.

"No school. But it is Sunday."

"Oh . . . yeah."

"You got heaps of sleep last night. How 'bout wakin' up and going to church with me?"

"But I have to go to school tomorrow." Matt opened his eyes. "Can I just have one day to chill?"

"How about we go and pray about Wrinkles today?"

Matt's gut twisted. For a few moments, Wrinkles's disappearance hadn't entered his mind. Now the empty feeling returned. He sat up and nodded.

"I guess I can go with you this morning," Matt said.

"You never know how God is working," Grandpa said. "Let's go, and maybe He'll tell us."

Matt turned his feet to the side of the bed and flipped the covers away.

Grandpa backed away and gave him room. "I'll see you downstairs. How about biscuits for breakfast?"

"Sure, Grandpa. That'd be good."

○○○○○

Matt followed Grandpa into one of the pews on the left side of the church sanctuary. The smooth wood of the bench felt cool to his touch as he sat down. Grandpa's arm moved to rest on the back of the pew behind him. Calming music flowed from the keyboards as everyone entered.

Mom and Dad had decided to attend a later service. For now, it was just him and his grandfather sitting together.

The church wasn't crowded this morning. Maybe a lot of people were on vacation. In a way, the smaller group made things more personal. Like the service would have special meaning for him.

After the music, Pastor Britt stood at the front of the gathering to begin his message.

"The story of the Good Shepherd is one we can all take comfort in," the pastor said. His soft voice calmed them. "The story begins when one lamb wanders away from the flock and is lost."

How scary to be lost.

That sheep had lost its way and didn't know what direction to head in. It could have been dark and maybe cold. Maybe the sheep had tripped on the rocks and fallen. It would be hurt and injured.

"But the Good Shepherd cared enough about that one sheep that he left the whole flock and went searching for the lamb who had wandered away," the pastor continued.

Whoa. That was cool. Matt had felt kind of lost before he found faith.

Matt had wondered about a lot of things. How the Earth was made. What happened after we died. Where did God live. Where was heaven. Things had become clearer when he'd understood that God created everyone and everything. God lived in heaven, and when we believed in Jesus, we had a special home with Him there.

"How happy the Shepherd was when he found that one lost sheep!" the pastor exclaimed. "And I guess the sheep was happy too—" Soft laughter came from around the church.

"It's a lesson for all of us. That God cares for each one. He comes after us and searches until He finds us. He rescues us from loneliness and pain and hurt. That is the goodness of God."

Grandpa squeezed Matt's shoulder. The pastor continued, but Matt knew he'd already heard a message just for him.

God cared about the things that were happening. Like the Shepherd cared for the sheep, God would carry him when things got tough.

He'd pray to find Wrinkles. And trust that he'd find out the truth about what happened to his dog.

After the pastor said a closing prayer, Matt walked with Grandpa to the back exit.

Adrienne, a girl from school, stood next to the door handing out roses. She held one out to Grandpa. "Here, Mr. Harley."

"What's this for?"

"Just a reminder of the stained glass window—" Adrienne said. She lifted her eyes to a window above the door. "It's broken. Part of the rose is missing."

"You don't say?" Grandpa stopped and examined the window.

"When they blew up the train station, everything shook," Adrienne said.

"It broke the window?" Matt asked.

"Just a small part, but we're taking donations to replace it." She held out a rose. "Here Matt, you take one too."

Matt usually didn't carry flowers around, but he took one.

Grandpa stuck the rose in the button hole of his shirt pocket. "Thank you, Miss. I'll remember to bring a donation."

Matt held the flower loosely in his cupped hand. "Yeah, thanks." He had no idea what he'd do with it—maybe give it to Mom when he got home.

Grandpa and Matt exited the church and got into the Jeep.

"Say, Matt," Grandpa said. "Where's the nearest gas station? Looks like I need a fill-up."

Matt guided Grandpa to the new BP, and he got out. As Grandpa filled the tank, Matt twirled the rose in his hand. He had to admit, it was pretty and smelled good too. The petals were soft.

"Oops," Matt said. He'd handled the rose too much. The outside petals fell away, revealing a shiny inner bud. Only it didn't exactly look like a part of the flower. Matt peeled away more of the blossom until he'd uncovered the center. There, nestled within the soft petals of the rose, sat another ruby!

He'd followed the fifth message of wisdom in Scotland, so he shouldn't be surprised that another ruby would appear.

With Jasper imprisoned, how would another trip to Koinopia help him? Jasper wouldn't be there to guide him.

Matt slipped the ruby into the pocket of his jeans. He'd keep it safe for a time to come. But first, he had to rescue his friend.

CHAPTER TWENTY-ONE

DISCOVERY

Matt arrived home after church and joined his mother in the kitchen.

"Hey, Matt," Mom greeted him. "We're about to do the laundry from our trip. Anything to add?"

Matt wrinkled his nose. "Yeah—sure. Just about my whole suitcase." He opened the refrigerator, hoping to find a quick snack.

"Good thing I got the clothes from your backpack before it was stolen."

Matt started to grab a bottle of orange juice. "The clothes in my backpack?" He turned. He wasn't sure that he'd heard her right.

"Yeah, they were in the bottom. Don't you remember the spare clothes you brought—in case our luggage got lost? And there was a pair of socks."

"You got the clothes and socks out of my backpack *before* we went to Loch Ness?"

"Yeah." She looked confused. "The socks were kind of heavy. Did you save shells from the beach in them? From our day at the sea?"

"Mom! I love you!" Matt stepped over and hugged her hard. "*What?*"

"Listen, Mom. Those socks are important!" Matt's heart pounded. "They have some of my souvenirs." *The Stones of Fire!*

She frowned. "We haven't washed anything yet. They're in the laundry room."

Matt skimmed around the corner into the laundry room. Piles of clothes had been separated and lay on the floor. Matt went through them, tossing shorts, pajamas, and Dad's swimsuit to the side. No socks.

Had Dad already started doing the laundry?

Matt opened the top of the washer. Lots of dark clothes lay in a wet circle, but no white socks.

Wonder if they're in the dryer? His stomach ached. He could just imagine the Stones of Fire banging around and around in the dryer. If they got cracked, would they still help Jasper? Matt bent to look inside the dryer.

"Matt?" Dad stood in the kitchen holding a basket of clothes. He peered into the laundry room and quirked an eye. "You're doing laundry now?"

"He left some souvenirs in a pair of socks," Mom said.

Matt couldn't contain his excitement. "Dad! I need to look through that basket!"

"All of a sudden, I'm the king of England," Dad said. "I didn't know laundry was so important." He laughed. "Help yourself."

His parents stood watching him look through the basket of clothes, then Mom turned back to the kitchen.

"I'll call animal control and tell them about Wrinkles, then let's have lunch."

Dad followed her. "Good idea. And grilled cheese sounds good to me."

Matt didn't care that his parents might think he was a little crazy. He put aside some T-shirts, shorts, and a beach towel.

Then Matt saw them. His socks. The pair in which he'd hidden the Stones of Fire. The pair he'd thought were stolen by Balmore. The pair he'd jumped into the freezing lake to save. But they hadn't been in his backpack. Mom had taken them out before their trip to Loch Ness.

His hands shook as he patted the foot of the socks and then reached inside. The perfect, round stones were still there! Matt looked over his shoulder. Mom and Dad were busy with lunch. He took the Stones up to his room.

⬡⬡⬡⬡⬡

A new spark of hope ignited inside of Matt as he shook the white orbs out of the socks and onto his bed. They sparkled in the light coming through his bedroom window.

The Stones of Fire could free Jasper. Matt had to rescue his friend! But he had to find Wrinkles too! He said a prayer for God's help.

Matt slipped on his hoodie and zipped the two Stones in the front pocket. He hurried downstairs and opened the front door of the house.

"Matt?" Mom caught him.

"Got to search for Wrinkles, Mom."

"Be careful and check in."

"I'll be gone a while, but I've got my watch. I'll text." Matt closed the door behind him.

Julie came up the street on her bike and spotted Matt. She curved toward him on the front circle drive. "Hey, Matt!" She stopped beside him and parked her bike. "Do you have them? Did you find the Stones of Fire?"

Matt nodded and a smile spread on his face. He motioned to Julie and she followed him. He hurried around the corner of the house and stopped under the cedar tree. When they were safely out of sight, he unzipped the hoodie pocket and brought out the Stones of Fire.

"I found them." He gazed at the round stones, opaque now, but shimmering with the beauty of glistening moonstones. "But I barely escaped the Druids."

"Oh, Matt! They're beautiful!" Julie's eyes widened. "What about the fire?"

"The fire is within. The Stones erupt like a volcano—when the time is right." Matt let Julie gaze for a moment, then returned the Stones of Fire to his pocket.

Julie looked different, somehow. The front of her hair had been pulled back in braids, and the rest hung around her shoulders. She seemed more like the high school girls—older. They stood silent for a moment.

"Sorry you came home to find Wrinkles gone," Julie finally said.

Matt nodded. "I'm headed out to find him." He strode toward the backyard.

Julie trailed behind him to the garage. "Don't worry! He'll probably come trotting up like he's had a big adventure."

Grandpa's jeep sat parked next to the garage. Something had been pushed into the bushes nearby,

"What's that in the bushes?"

"It's Ryan's four-wheeler," Julie said.

Matt ran over to check it out. "How'd it get in there?"

She appeared beside him. "I kind of pushed it."

"What?"

"So his parents wouldn't know Ryan never made it to basketball camp."

Matt scowled. "Tell me fast."

"Ryan is at the Rim," Julie started to explain.

"The Rim? But how?" Matt's eye twitched.

"Remember Starling?"

"Yeah, Miss Duncan's bird."

"Starling told me Ryan accidentally ate the Wonder Wafer he'd saved."

"The bird *talked?*"

Julie nodded. "Yeah, and he's got attitude."

"Ryan should have saved the Wonder Wafer for me. Now how will I go to the Rim?" Matt placed a palm on his forehead. "Anything else I should know?"

Julie leaned back against the jeep. "Ryan's family thinks he's at basketball camp. Coach Bryson and the other guys get back tonight! If Ryan doesn't return with them—"

"His mom will go ballistic. And the town will be in a panic!" Matt started pacing. "They'll think he's been kidnapped!" Julie's mouth dropped open and she covered it with her hand.

"I thought things were going to get easier." Matt shook his head. "But now I have to take the Stones of Fire to Jasper, find Wrinkles, and get Ryan home tonight before his parents figure out he's missing!"

Silence settled between them.

"Time doesn't stop at the Rim," Julie crossed her arms.

Matt didn't want to hear any more bad news. A dark bird flew from the cedar tree and swooped into the garage.

"*ACK!*"

"It's Starling!" Julie said. She ran into the garage, and Matt followed. Starling landed on the tool bench and ruffled his feathers.

"Where did you come from?" Julie asked. "I guess you've been eavesdropping."

"*ACK!* I like to listen in," Starling croaked.

"It's crazy to be talking to a bird," Matt said.

"I talk only when necessary." Starling cocked his head and stared at Matt. "It's a knack humans might learn."

"So what have you got to say?" Julie asked.

"*ACK!*" Starling croaked again.

"Spill," Julie said.

"I don't have to," Starling cawed. "Ryan already has." He drifted down to the floor.

Crumbs lay beside the tool bench. Matt bent and picked up a large piece and turned it over. Shiny frosting coated the other side.

"Pieces of Wonder Wafer," Matt said. "Ryan must have dropped some before he was zapped to the Rim."

"Think that will be enough?" Julie knelt next to him to inspect the crumbs.

"Let's hope so," Matt said. "These bites of wafer will take me to the Rim . . . and I have to go now. Will you keep looking for Wrinkles for me?" He stood.

"But won't your parents miss you?" Julie pushed up from the floor.

"I've already told Mom I'm going to search for Wrinkles. Maybe I can get back before it's too late."

"Be careful, Matt." Julie's eyes glistened.

"I will." He said, nodding. "You should probably head out. I have no idea what will happen when I eat that wafer."

She nodded. "I'm going home now. I'll search for Wrinkles on the way."

Matt walked Julie to her bike and waved as she pedaled off.

◇◇◇◇◇

So this was it. Matt patted the front of his hoodie. The Stones of Fire rested safely inside, and he'd stowed the sixth ruby in his jeans' pocket.

He picked up a piece of wafer and blew it off. What would happen after he ate it? In Koinopia, it'd been a delicious treat that gave a lot of strength. But here, it would affect him differently. He said a prayer, then lifted the bit of wafer into his mouth.

It tasted zingy and delicious—just like in Koinopia. Then a strange sensation came over him. His muscles tensed and stretched. He whirled around the garage, going mega-fast. Everything blurred together. He flew up to the ceiling and around the walls. *When* would it stop? He whirled into a corner. Grandpa's camping lantern crashed to the floor. Mom's pie pans flew across the garage like frisbees. A cat yowled from the outside. The walls of the garage parted and everything blinked dark.

WHOA!!

Light appeared at the horizon of his vision. A fiery light. Orange and yellow blazes. Was something burning?

He closed his eyes and opened them again. He could see stubbly tree limbs jutting in every direction just above his head. Prickly bushes surrounded him, like he'd landed in an overgrown field of weeds and bushy plants. An ashy smell rushed into his nostrils, and he coughed.

So this must be the Rim.

CHAPTER TWENTY-TWO

PREDATOR

Dawdle skimmed on his belly around the surface of the Glops. He swished his tail side-to-side, maneuvering through the short, stubby trees.

Ryan followed behind, careful not to lose his balance. It felt like walking around in a boat while waves rolled underneath, and the smoky air made it hard to breathe.

"I think the prickleberries are just ahead," Dawdle said. He finally stopped next to a bush with half-opened leaves. Dawdle reached for a leaf and opened it with his paw.

He flinched and sat up on his hind legs. "I could have pricked myself."

Ryan came forward and examined Dawdle's paw. He turned it over. "You did!" Bright red oozed out of Dawdle's nicked skin.

Dawdle pulled back his paw and rubbed the scratched place along his side. "I might have forgotten to tell you. You could watch out for the prickles while you're picking the berries."

Ryan's face paled. He didn't like the sight of blood. And Dawdle had some scars along his arm.

"Looks like you've been pricked before."

"Maybe a lot of times," Dawdle said. "But I seem to get used to it. The pricks don't bother me as much as they used to."

"Why don't you quit eating prickleberries? Man, they hurt you!" Ryan shook his head. "Isn't there any other food around here?"

"There might be." Dawdle looked toward the Woodlands. "Edible plants are near there. But I think it is a lot of work to harvest them." He gazed over at the stand of Pricklebushes. "To stay here is easier."

Ryan frowned. He couldn't wait to get home.

It was if Dawdle were awake but still sleeping somehow. He wasn't sure about anything. He glided around without any purpose. He even ignored hurtful things and didn't stop doing them. Dawdle seemed satisfied with dreary things and had lost any excitement—if he'd ever had any.

Ryan's stomach growled. He needed to eat. The pale prickleberries kind of looked like the berries at the farmer's market at home.

"You do want to try some?" Dawdle opened his hand. He'd managed to harvest a few berries without getting pricked again.

"Thanks, man. I'll find my own." Ryan brushed the top of the leaves with his hand. One leaf seemed bigger than the others, and a big berry hung underneath. "Sweet!" He carefully avoided a thorn and plucked the fruit.

The berry had a little pink color, at least. He popped it in his mouth. A syrupy taste met his tongue. Maybe prickleberries wouldn't be so bad after all. And if the syrup was like honey, he'd have enough energy to make it to the Woodlands and find help.

◇◇◇◇◇

Matt had trouble standing up. Since he'd landed at the Rim, the annoying pink surface slowed his pace. How would he ever find Ryan? And what about Jasper? He patted the Stones of Fire in his hoodie pocket. At least he'd kept his clothes on when the Wonder Wafers had whirled him around in the garage. But finding Jasper would be slow-going, and he didn't have much time.

Matt struggled forward like he was walking in sludge. Where was he anyway? He'd headed toward the fiery light of the horizon. Now that it was a bit lighter, he could see more.

Pink mounds and deep pockmarks made it seem like everything had sunk into a big wad of bubble gum. The Rim had a weird sun, like a dim light turned on in a closet.

How many hours did he have to find Ryan and get back to Baywood? It had been one o'clock in the afternoon when he left home. He checked his watch. It still showed the same time so the watch must not be working! How would he text his parents?

Matt trudged ahead, knowing his time must be growing short. The dimness made him feel woozy and seemed to sap his strength.

"*G-R-R-R-R!*" A bellow erupted from the trees behind him.

Matt froze. Was it some kind of predator? Had the Wolvin tracked him down? His eye quivered. He ducked behind a stubbly tree and crumpled to the ground.

"*RRRARR!*"

That didn't sound like the Wolvin. What other kind of creature stalked him?

Matt curled into a ball and tucked his head into his knees. A wet, slobbery something landed on his neck.

It's going to eat me!

If the creature devoured him, would it feel like being swallowed by a whale or squeezed by an octopus? But the thing didn't swallow him. Instead, a slippery tongue thumped up and down on his head.

Matt opened one eye and peeped. A pink tongue the size of a surfboard flopped in front of him. He opened the other eye.

Two brown eyes as big as dinner plates danced in front of him. The nose twitched. The wavy coat bristled.

Matt struggled to his feet and took two steps back. He cracked a smile, then a big grin spread over his face.

The creature in front of him was huge. It was hairy. It had the smell of an afternoon wallow in damp leaves.

It was Wrinkles! He'd found his dog!

Wrinkles must have eaten some of the Wonder Wafers in the garage. Grandpa thought he'd run away. But Wrinkles had been zapped to the Rim! And it had changed him—in a big way.

This Wrinkles was huge. Matt stood only as tall as one of Wrinkles's legs. Matt grabbed the closest leg and wrapped his arms around it in a hug.

"*RRRUFFF!*" Wrinkles bellowed and licked his head. The huge tongue covered his head, but Matt didn't care.

"Hey, boy!" Matt smoothed his hair back into place. He patted Wrinkles's belly, only this time he had to jump up and give him a high-five on his stomach.

Wrinkles trotted away and started circling Matt faster and faster—just like he did in the yard when he was happy. The spongy surface rippled and rolled.

Matt rode the ripples and wished he had a ball to throw to Wrinkles. But what size would it have to be?

Julie had been right about one thing. Wrinkles grinned as if he'd been on a big adventure. He probably liked being huge. Did this mean Wrinkles was now the boss?

Wrinkles had been to obedience school. But would he still obey when Matt motioned to him? If he walked ahead and called Wrinkles, would his dog follow? He'd try it out.

Matt trudged forward through the spongy surface. "Come on, boy."

Wrinkles's panting seemed further behind. His dog wasn't following him. Matt stopped and turned. Wrinkles sat where Matt had left him.

Matt retreated a couple of steps. "Here, Wrinkles." Matt slapped his thigh.

Wrinkle sat.

Matt walked closer to him. "Here, boy."

"*RRUFF!*" Wrinkles answered but still sat.

What can I do now?

Wrinkles dropped his back and sat his rump on the ground. Then he pushed his front legs forward and bowed his head. Like he wanted Matt to climb up his leg.

Matt started up one leg, and Wrinkles bowed his head further. Matt clung to the rough skin and climbed to his neck. Wrinkles still had his collar on. Matt skimmed around the collar and positioned his legs underneath. He sat behind Wrinkles's head.

Wrinkles lifted his head, stood, and barked.

Matt covered his ears. The bark was loud but happy. Did Wrinkles want to carry him? Could Matt ride on his back?

As if reading his mind, Wrinkles trotted forward. Matt slipped to the side.

"Whoa!"

Wrinkles stopped and chuffed.

Matt scooted back to his place behind Wrinkles's collar.

"Okay, boy. I've got the idea. Only slower this time."

Wrinkles walked ahead. Matt seemed to get the rhythm of the whole thing. He patted Wrinkles's neck. His best dog began trotting, and Matt held on to the collar as Wrinkles forged ahead.

The spongy surface didn't slow them down. Matt glanced at the pink ground. Wrinkles's claws grabbed on and gave them traction.

All of a sudden, things didn't seem so dim. The Rim hadn't changed, but finding Wrinkles had given Matt hope.

"All right, boy. Let's find Ryan!"

Wrinkles sped faster as if he understood. Matt held on tight and searched across the gloppy mounds as Wrinkles swept over the surface, racing like an airboat through a swampy glade.

○○○○○○

Matt and Wrinkles threaded their way through the stubby trees and thorny bushes of the Rim, searching for Ryan. Wrinkles jumped whenever a hole burped open in the pink surface. They glided over slippery parts and skimmed around mounds of glop.

"Ry-an!" Matt called for the umpteenth time. "Hey, Ryan! I've come to take you back!" Matt checked side to side, searching the open areas and shadowed places of the Rim. The dreary scenery hadn't changed, but it seemed like they drew closer to the fire he'd first seen on the horizon. The blaze appeared taller now, and smoke stung his nose.

"Hey, Matt."

Matt jumped. A human voice had answered, although it didn't really sound like Ryan. Wrinkles stopped and whimpered. He'd heard it too.

Matt patted Wrinkles's neck. His dog sat and stretched out his front legs. Matt let go of the collar and slid down one of Wrinkles's legs. He brushed dust from his hands and walked to the place where he'd heard a voice. A clump of bushes encircled a small pond.

"What's up?"

Matt turned.

Ryan stood beside a jagged rip in the spongy surface. His face showed little emotion.

"Ryan! I've found you!" Matt laughed.

"You were looking for me?"

"Well, ye-ah." Matt tilted his head. "I came to take you with me."

Ryan looked from Matt to Wrinkles. "Where?"

"You know. Home!"

Matt studied his friend. Something had changed.

"Why should I want to go there?" Ryan shrugged. "I'm perfectly happy here."

Pink stains circled Ryan's mouth.

"Have you been eating something?"

"Just these berries. Dawdle brought me here. But . . . he's not here now."

Dawdle? Matt didn't know who Ryan's new friend was, but if he was from this dizzying place, the name fit.

Matt brushed his hand over the bushes surrounding the pond. Pale pink fruit fell to the ground. "Have those berries changed you? It's like you're in a daze."

"No, it's cool. No worries."

"There's plenty of worries!" Matt shouted. "Remember? You're supposed to be at ball camp, and you've got to return home before your family misses you!"

Ryan sat on a mound of glop. "My family." Matt thought he saw a spark in Ryan's eyes.

"Yeah. Home—where the people live who love you." Matt patted the sides of Ryan's cheeks. "Wake up!"

"Hmm?" Ryan squinted.

"And don't forget Jasper! We've got to rescue him!" Matt said. "He's in prison and he's depending on us."

How did Ryan get in this kind of shape? This was almost as bad as when the Starblades video game had hypnotized him.

Miss Duncan had told them the Skinks confuse and delay the Earples seeking to enter Koinopia.

And Ryan *was* confused. And he'd been delayed. If it were up to him, he might stay here forever. He didn't even want to go home or help Jasper. How could he light a fire under Ryan and get him to move forward?

Wrinkles barked, and Matt thought of something.

"Hey, Ryan."

"Hmm?"

"Why don't we go look for more of those berries? Maybe there's more ahead."

Ryan's dazed eyes stared at him. "A-ight."

"Wrinkles can carry both of us. He'll have us there in no time."

"Wrinkles?"

Wrinkles lowered his huge head and knelt. Matt patted his nose. "You remember him, my dog?"

"Dude's bigger."

"Yeah. And Wrinkles is faster. Come on!"

Matt climbed up a leg. "See? Like this."

Ryan followed, although not fast. Matt settled on Wrinkles's back and prayed Ryan would hurry. He finally appeared next to Matt.

"You've got to hang on to the collar." Matt showed Ryan how to slip his feet and legs under the collar—like a seat belt, and then hang on. "Wrinkles travel fast."

"Yeah. Okay." Ryan did as Matt instructed, and Matt couldn't have been more relieved.

He gripped Wrinkles's collar and patted his neck.

"Let's go, boy!"

Wrinkles scampered over the Glops, his claws catching hold and flying over the swampy surface.

Ryan patted Matt's leg. He turned to his friend. Ryan looked sick.

"Whoa, Wrinkles!"

Ryan pushed away from Wrinkles's collar and slid down his leg. His feet touched the ground, and he puked his guts out.

The prickleberries were history. Maybe Ryan would snap out of it.

Chapter Twenty-Three

BONFIRE

"The bonfire burns." Noris raised his head above the rock he'd hidden behind. He spied on the Wolvin gathering below. The wolfish creatures stood together, murmuring low and erupting in howls. Others scampered low to the ground, gathering limbs for the mounting flames. Smoke rose from the fire, stinging his eyes.

"'Tis a strange fire," Juman said from beside him. "The smell of it reminds me of a burial wreath."

"Aye," Noris said. "And the smell is not the only strange thing."

One of the Wolvin began turning in a hypnotic dance, its hairy arms raised and head tilted back. A long howl escaped its lips.

"And they are not afraid of the fire," Juman shook his head. "Wolves usually run away from flames and smoke. But this fire seems to incite them."

"To a frenzy." Noris regarded his friend. "They be a strange breed." He scooted back downhill from the rock and stood. "We must find Bounded Hollow!"

"We'll keep searching." Juman moved down the slope and returned to his horse.

"Let us be off, then," Noris said.

They quietly led their horses away from the Wolvin gathering. Noris mounted his steed. Juman did the same. They bolted around the rocks and black sediment of the Rim.

Noris's heart sank. They'd searched the Rim for hours, yet the prison of Bounded Hollow eluded them. He longed for the safety of the Woodlands, to be hidden among the ancient trees of his flourishing home.

Petrus could be imprisoned beneath their very feet in an ancient tunnel sculpted by eons of flowing water. The pale light of the Rim's moon did not help. Noris searched the dark outline of boulders and outcroppings. *My friend, where could you be?*

His horse reared, pummeling the air with his front legs.

"Whoa, Vagabond!" Noris shifted, keeping his seat on the horse.

Juman's steed answered with a whinnying cry and shook its head. Juman pulled the reins close. "Ho, Banner. Easy lad."

The earth rumbled beneath them.

"Make haste! A herd rushes upon us!" Noris guided his horse off the path toward a circle of boulders.

Juman followed but looked around them. "There is no dust rising. Or hooves galloping."

They hid within the circle and dismounted, soothing the horses.

The ground rumbled once more.

"That is not my imagining," Noris said. He sought Juman's eyes for an answer.

Juman shrugged. "If it is, I am imagining too."

A large shadow appeared against a boulder across the way. A head, perhaps. And stout body. Taller than the boulder.

"*GRRRRR!*"

Noris jumped. A rumpled body with nose, ears, and eyes approached them. And a voice came from behind the creature's head.

"What is it, Wrinkles?"

Noris stared. The voice sounded familiar. Was it? Could it be? Young Silvers came into view as the creature walked near. Thank the saintly stars!

Noris rose from his place and ran to the path. "Lad!"

"Huh?" The lad's eyes grew wide, searching the dim light.

"Here, young Matthew!" Noris waved his hands wide.

A frown, then a smile spread upon the boy's face.

"Noris?" Matt Silvers patted the creature's neck, and the hound bent low. The young Valenian skimmed down one leg and came near. "I'm so glad we found you," Matt breathed out.

"Aye, as are we," Noris said. "All Valenians are needed in this battle. Your own self being one of us!"

Above them, another boy sat on the creature. "You have a friend?" Noris asked.

"Yes, but this crazy place has made him—not himself." Matt turned. Ryan had dozed off after becoming sick. Maybe it was a side-effect of the prickleberries.

"And where is the Guardian?" Noris searched behind the dog creature.

Matt's face clouded. "He is in prison—kidnapped by the Wolvin."

"It is worse than I feared!" Noris bellowed. "The same fate has befallen Petrus!"

"We can't lose them!" Matt said. "Do you know your way around the Rim?"

"We have fought many battles here."

Juman joined them. "This is your steed, lad?"

"Not a steed—a dog. My pet."

"Hounds are much bigger in your world," Juman said.

"Not when we're at home. He's just a regular dog," Matt said. "But a few bites of Wonder Wafer changed him."

"Koinopia has that effect on the natural world," Juman said. "Just a small bit of that kingdom can bring change—in a huge way. May I offer counsel?"

"We are waiting, holding our breath," Noris crossed his arms.

Juman's voice calmed them. "We must band together. With our knowledge of the Rim and Matt's special gifts and huge canine—we have a better chance of finding them both."

"Perhaps the Eternal One has kept Jasper and Petrus together," Noris bowed his head. "At least they may not be alone."

"Your dog has a keen nose?" Juman asked.

"Not as good as a retriever," Matt answered. "But yeah, he sniffs things out."

Juman's eyes met Noris's. He nodded. They were thinking the same thing.

"Then perhaps he can find Petrus!" Noris returned to his horse and pulled the small horn and scarf from his pack. "These belong to him."

"I'd try just about anything!" Matt said. "Maybe he can track the scent!"

Noris rushed to Matt and handed him the scarf. Matt lifted it to his dog's nose.

The dog creature inhaled deeply through his nose.

"*RRUFF!*"

"I think he knows what we want," young Silvers said. He climbed the dog and settled behind the collar.

Noris and Juman returned to their horses. When they were mounted, Noris looked up and nodded. "We will follow you, young Valenian!"

Matt patted his dog. "C'mon, boy. Take us to Petrus and Jasper! Let's go!"

○○○○○○

Jasper tossed his woolen cloak across the damp floor of the cold chamber. Petrus had need of it. The Valenian prince had coughed through the night. And it didn't help that the acrid smell of smoke and the taste of ash penetrated the passageway that led to their small space.

"You keep the cloak," Petrus said. "No reason for both of us to be sick."

"But your coughs are much worse." Compassion welled up in Jasper's heart. "It would help if you kept warm."

"It is only a matter of minutes now, anyway," Petrus whispered. "They will soon come for us." He closed his eyes.

"Stay with me, Petrus. Our rescuers will arrive. Do not lose hope."

Jasper jerked his shackles. The chains pulled taunt, and crumbles of rock fell beside him. Jasper examined the wall. The iron plate to which his chains were fastened had pulled away from the rock. If he kept tugging, the plate might come out all the way.

If only he had the strength of a child! But he'd lived on watery gruel for weeks. His strength had drained away. He doubted if he could even stand.

"*Woof-woooo!*" A howl echoed into their chamber from the passageway.

"*Woof-woooo!*" Another cry joined the first.

"*Woof-woof-wooo!*" A third Wolvin joined in.

Petrus opened his eyes, and for the first time, Jasper saw fear.

"They are here," Petrus said.

Fury entered with a flaming torch, and two others followed. They danced between Jasper and Petrus, tails curling behind them. The gray Wolvin opened their mouths wide, revealing sharp fangs and teeth.

"This one might be tasty," one of the Wolvin growled. He lifted Petrus's frail arm.

"Don't touch him, Devon!" Fury shouted, his smelly breath seething from his chest. "We parade the Guardian through the prison first! Then on to the bonfire with both of them!"

CHAPTER TWENTY-FOUR

LIZARDVILLE

"*Rat-a-tat-tat!*"

Julie looked up from her spot on the leather couch. The sharp pecks on the window could only mean one thing. Starling had come to visit.

She opened the slats on the living room shutters.

"*ACK!*" Outside, Starling flew to a magnolia tree and jumped from one branch to another, flapping his wings.

Crazy bird!

She glanced around the living room and into the kitchen. No one else seemed to be around. That was good because if Starling swooped in and started yakking, Mom would probably faint.

Julie slid across the wood floor in her socks. She cracked open the front door. Humid air breezed inside, reminding her that it was spring.

Starling swooped down and suspended himself in front of the porch.

"Got to come now! *ACK!*"

Julie stepped into her flip-flops and squeezed out the door, shutting it behind her.

"I've already got one emergency! Wrinkles is missing!" She crossed her arms. "What's your hurry?"

"Oh, I don't know." Starling's crown feathers stood up. "Maybe it's because Baywood is Lizardville!"

Julie blew out a breath of frustration. "I got it. But what can I do?"

"Can you count to a hundred?" Starling eeked.

Julie smirked. "Of course I can!"

"That's how many Skinks will be turning over garbage cans in the morning!"

Julie looked up and down the street. Every house had set out a can for pickup the next day. She felt sick.

"They'll be leaving the old mill and branching out," Starling said, bristling, unless we stop them."

A squeaky bike chain interrupted Julie's thoughts. Wyatt pulled into her driveway.

"Hey, Jules."

Starling swept into the upper branches of the tree.

"How about going for a ride?" Wyatt stopped in front of her.

"Um," Julie started. "Can't go with you right now."

Wyatt frowned. "What's up?"

"Remember the lizards?"

"Ugh." Wyatt groaned. "They're back?"

She peered into the trees, then at Wyatt. Maybe he could help her more than Starling. At least Wyatt didn't have an attitude.

"They're at the old grist mill. Just outside of town," Julie said.

"Did someone report it or something?" Wyatt swung a leg off the bike and put down the kickstand.

Julie shook her head. "Probably wasn't reported yet."

"Well, maybe, you know, we should call animal control or something."

Julie hadn't thought of that. Why *didn't* she just tell the adults? But since the Skinks emerged from the Dark Void, would animal control really know how to get rid of them? She sat on the cool porch steps, and Wyatt joined her.

"Don't know if this will help . . . but back in California, we had trouble with peacocks."

"Peacocks?" Julie's eyes widened.

"Yeah. They hung out in the trees, yelled in the middle of the night, and, you know, left poop all over cars and stuff."

Julie wrinkled her nose. "So what'd they do?"

"Called a guy." Wyatt shrugged. "He came and got them with nets and took them off somewhere safe."

"Guess they were glad to get them moved," Julie said.

"Yeah, but some of the girls thought they were pretty." He sighed. "My mom even saved some peacock feathers."

What?

"Your *Mom* has peacock feathers?"

"Well, yeah." Wyatt smiled in that way that included his eyes. "Uses them in vases and stuff."

"Wyatt, can you get some of those feathers for me?"

The wind blew a wisp of hair across Julie's cheek, tickling her face. She smoothed the strand away.

Wyatt smiled. "I think I can find some. You're like, crafty?"

Julie nodded. "Maybe I can put them in my room."

"Sure, I'll ask her." He bit his bottom lip. "But what about those lizards?"

"*ACK!*"

"What's up with that bird?" Wyatt peered into the tree.

Julie glanced up. Starling flapped like a trapped butterfly. She knew what Starling wanted. But she didn't want to see the Skinks again! And she wasn't exactly dressed for fighting lizards. Wonder if one ran up her leg?

"You okay?" Wyatt searched her face.

"Yeah," Julie took a deep breath and let it out. "We could call animal control. But first, let's check out the old mill ourselves."

"Um, okay. Is it far?"

"Just outside of town. I'll ask my parents if I can go riding." She looked down at her shorts. "And I've got to get changed."

"Cool. I'll borrow my Mom's e-bike and come back," Wyatt said. "It'll be faster." He pedaled down the driveway and headed toward his house. Julie turned to go inside.

Starling rasped behind her. "*ACK!* You haven't got much time!"

⬡⬡⬡⬡⬡

Julie sat behind Wyatt as he zoomed through Baywood on the e-bike, passing Tinker's store and the Creamy Cone, then turning right at the courthouse square and heading out of town past the school and the Sub Shop.

Wyatt spoke over his shoulder. "How far is the old mill from here?"

"Keep going straight. The road gets narrower," Julie said. "I think it turns into gravel before we get there."

Wyatt's head bobbed like he understood.

It felt weird sitting behind Wyatt. Julie liked to ride her own bike, but this was faster, and they didn't have much time.

Tall trees grew close to the road and shaded them as they drew near to the old mill. The blacktop became gravel, and they bumped along the road. The way narrowed to a dirt path. Grass grew between tracks left by old wagons and pickups.

Wyatt stopped when the dirt tracks disappeared. "Yo. I think we've run out of road."

"Looks that way," Julie said. "But the mill is just ahead. When we had a school trip here, our bus parked, then we walked through some tall grass." She got off the bike and took off her helmet. Wyatt did the same.

"What's that sound?" Wyatt turned his head. "Is there water close by? You know, like a stream or something?"

"Yeah, the old mill is next to a creek." She listened. The rippling water soothed her nerves. The scent of honeysuckles drifted over from an old wire fence.

"Lead the way," Wyatt said. "I have no idea where to go."

Julie nodded. "Um, I don't want to scare you or anything, but watch out for snakes. We'll be going through some tall grass."

"Snakes?" Wyatt's face turned pale.

"They may not be out yet, but you never know." Julie didn't want to scare him, but she did want him to watch where he was going.

"Let's just get there, okay?"

She looked across the field and saw the tin roof of the grist mill reflecting the sun. "It's just over the next hill. I can see the top from here."

They hiked across a clearing, and the tall grass swished at Julie's knees. Over the next hill, the three-story grist mill stood next to a running creek. A big waterwheel stood beside the mill, submerged in the water a bit. The weathered-gray wheel was missing some blades.

Julie imagined that back in the day, a new red oak wheel captured the water of the creek and lifted the glistening stream until it flowed onto the other side, turning it in a circle.

They walked closer. Below them, the wheel rested in the water next to the rusty walls of the mill's first floor. The mill had windows, but they'd been boarded up. The second story had a porch going around it connecting a front and back door. A plank bridge led from the grass where they stood, over the water, to the front door.

Wyatt searched the ground. "I don't see any of those slimy things."

"Not yet," Julie said. "Let's look inside. I bet we can look through a crack in the wall."

"Let's head over to the porch." Wyatt took the lead and headed across the planked bridge. Julie followed.

"Check the wall," Julie said.

Wyatt nodded. "There's a crack." He pointed at a corner. "You want to look first?"

She froze. If there was a Skink on the other side, it might spit slime through the crack in her direction.

"No problem. I can look." Wyatt crouched down and peered through the crack. He raised up and looked even paler.

"There's at least a hundred." He exhaled. "But you can look. They're not close to this wall."

Julie bent to peer through the opening.

Across the large room, Skinks slithered and crept. The creatures glided across the floor, around wooden posts, and into piles of weeds and old sacks of corn meal.

Bile rose into her throat, and she gulped back the sting. She stood. "We've got to do something. Otherwise, the other stores and the homes in Baywood . . ." She didn't finish.

"Will look just like the Creamy Cone did," Wyatt finished.

Miss Duncan had said it was up to Julie to get rid of the Skinks, but this was over the top.

Julie's shoulders sagged. The Skinks were no ordinary lizards. They had to get those peacock feathers and ice water—and do it fast.

Chapter Twenty-Five

ENEMIES

Julie stood with Wyatt on the second-story porch of the old mill. Inside, the Skinks had gathered in clusters around mounds of weeds and old corn.

"Ugh. We've got to get rid of them."

"Let's do a search, " Wyatt said.

"What?"

"You never know what might turn up," Wyatt's eyebrows rose. He typed in a browser search on his phone. "How-to-get-rid-of-lizards."

Julie waited. "Well?"

"Says here lizards and peacocks are natural enemies."

"Hmm?"

"Peacocks sometimes eat them."

So that explains the peacock feathers!

He shut his phone. "Lizards are scared of them," Wyatt mused. "So, you know, they might be scared of their feathers too."

"It's worth a try," Julie said. *And probably the only thing that will work.*

Wyatt was on a roll. "And since they're kind of like snakes, they don't like the cold either."

Julie nodded. "Yeah, they're reptiles. The cold slows them down."

"We have dry ice at the Creamy Cone and inside our delivery truck. And those feathers are at my house," Wyatt adjusted his ball cap. "I'd say we don't have time to waste."

"I'm thinking the same," Julie said.

She couldn't believe Wyatt had come up with this on his own. She didn't even have to explain the Dark Void or that the "lizards" were actually the Skinks and that Queen Anne from Koinopia had said the same things.

Wyatt stuck up his index finger. "I've got an idea. "Mom's still mad about the mess they made at the shop, so she'll want to help us. I can text her and have her bring the delivery truck and the peacock feathers."

"Think she can find her way out here?"

Wyatt looked up as if he were puzzling something out. "I'll send her the location. We can meet her at the blacktop road."

✧✧✧✧✧✧

Slizard slid onto the warm hood of an abandoned truck and surveyed the Skinks below. They'd munched and fed around the old grist mill all day. It was about time they worked off all that grazing.

He'd heard from the Wolvin and couldn't wait to share the news with his underlings. He shot out his long tongue and snapped it over their heads. The snap brought the Skinks to attention like the cracking of a whip.

"Skinks of the Dark Void!" Slizard hissed loud and long. His collar puffed up around his head like a fiery halo. He raised up on his legs and swirled his tail behind him, knocking aside the underlings who dared to approach him from behind.

"Gather!"

The Skinks emerged from all corners of the mill. They scampered from old bags and up from the rotting floor, slid down through the wooden ceiling, and poked out their heads from knot holes and old barrels. Skinks erupted from behind the old mill's crushing stone, and the females abandoned the eggs in their nests to join the others.

"I have news," Slizard said, dead-calm. The rest of the Skinks grew quiet. "Our great enemy, the Guardian—I will not say his name," Slizard hissed. "He is at this moment," Slizard paused, then shouted, "headed toward the bonfires!"

A great hissing arose from the pile of Skinks, and long, slimy tails swerved and curled like a pit of snakes.

"The Skinks have triumphed where the Craevin failed!" Slizard proclaimed victory.

Skinks ran up and down the old posts, scampered around the millstone, and did push-ups against the creaking floor, celebrating their victory with snapping tongues.

"Freeze!" Slizard's tail whipped around, sending the smaller Skinks to the floor.

The under-Skinks stopped the celebration. Just the mention of cold brought to mind crippling ice. They halted.

"We're not finished in Baywood. The Guardian is ours, but the town of Baywood must pay for delaying the Dweller's will! We'll spread our slime and have them so confused chaos will rule!"

A red tongue shot out from the crowd. "We invaded the ice cream shop! We have them on the run!"

A tail curled around an abandoned sack of meal. A Skink head appeared. "The tall girl. She knows about us. She is aligned with the yellow beaks that attacked us."

"And Matt Silvers!" another Skink shouted.

"A small matter." Slizard's eyes glowed. "The girl is only a *friend* of Matt Silvers. She has no power of her own. In fact—" His collar puffed larger. "She is afraid of us."

A Skink perched, stock-still, on a mill sack. "So, what is your plan?"

"We attack the streets of Baywood next." Slizard turned in a circle around a tall post. "Aw, the luscious leftovers in those garbage cans," he hissed. "It is all yours. Plus any beetled insects you wish to devour."

"Make ready!" Slizard roared. "We invade the streets of Baywood tonight!"

Chapter Twenty-Six

ATTACK PLAN

Julie jumped off of Wyatt's bike. Her bottom ached. The ride back from the grist mill had been bumpy, but they finally returned to the blacktop. Now, they could only wait for Wyatt's mother to arrive.

They didn't have long to wait. The Creamy Cone delivery truck zoomed over the hill, rumbling and rocking side to side. At first, Mrs. Sawyer didn't see them until Wyatt signaled and rang the bike bell.

Julie waved wildly. "Over here!"

The Creamy Cone van pulled to the side, brakes hissing and stinky exhaust escaping out the tailpipe.

Pop! Black smoke blew out the back of the van.

Mrs. Sawyer waved through the windshield. The engine turned off, and the driver's door cracked open.

"Wyatt!" Mrs. Sawyer got out. She wore dark sunglasses under her white ball cap. Her blonde hair hung behind in a ponytail.

Wyatt met her as she came around the truck.

"Glad you're all right," Mrs. Sawyer said. "Where are those creatures?"

Mrs. Sawyer hadn't called them lizards. Even Wyatt's mom knew there was something not normal about them. Maybe because she'd had that crazy spell when she'd been slimed during the Creamy Cone attack.

"They're at the old grist mill," Julie said. "Just past the gravel and dirt roads."

"We need ice," Wyatt said.

"We received a delivery of ice a few days ago." Mrs. Sawyer took off her glasses and peered at Wyatt. "Now, *how* are you going to use it?"

Wyatt glanced at Julie. "Well, you know, we haven't exactly figured that out."

Julie jumped in. "Wyatt figured out that since they're reptiles, ice water will slow them down." She paused. "And lizards are afraid of peacocks."

Mrs. Wyatt nodded. "What we need is a plan."

"A plan?" Julie asked.

"You know, a strategy," Mrs. Sawyer said.

Wyatt turned to Julie. "Mom was in the military."

"Oh."

"Four years at Travis Air Force Base," Mrs. Sawyer said. "I need a recon report."

"Hmm?" Julie tilted her head.

"She needs to know the layout of the building," Wyatt explained. "You know, where the doors and windows are, the way the water wheel has an opening—"

"Water wheel?" Mrs. Sawyer creased her brow. "That could be a challenge. Hang on." She jumped back into the truck and returned with a Sharpie and a long, yellow pad of paper. "Let's draw out a plan. Then we'll head to the mill."

○○○○○○

Julie sat squeezed between Wyatt and his mother as the Creamy Cone truck left the blacktop and returned to the mill. They bumped over the gravel road and the van lurched when it hit a pothole in the dirt track.

"Careful, Mom," Wyatt said from across the front seat. "This road hasn't been traveled on in like, fifty years."

"Not exactly a road anymore," Julie said.

"And old C.C.'s not exactly in great shape." She grinned and patted the dashboard.

"C.C.?" Julie asked.

"Mom's nickname for the truck," Wyatt shrugged. "Acronym for Creamy Cone."

"But she gets the job done," Mrs. Sawyer said. "Oh, what's that?" She stomped the brakes then turned the steering wheel fast.

Whop! A sharp boulder blocked their path, but they'd turned just in time to miss it—almost. It smacked the side of the truck.

Mrs. Sawyer shook her head. "These brakes! That didn't sound good."

"The mill's just over the next hill," Julie said. There's a tree there. You can park behind it."

"No use blowing our cover," Wyatt added.

C.C. crested the hill then rolled halfway down. Mrs. Sawyer parked the truck next to the tree, behind a low-hanging limb.

Wyatt jumped out of the truck and helped Julie down.

Mrs. Sawyer came around from the other side. "Ready to do this?" She got out the pad and studied Julie's sketch of the mill.

"First, we're going to float some ice around that water wheel." She peered in the direction of the wheel. "I can see there's a wooden channel enclosing the wheel. We'll float the ice in there."

"That should keep them from escaping through the water," Wyatt said.

"Right."

"What about the doors? Can't they go under them?" Julie asked.

Mrs. Sawyer frowned. "We need a second way of stopping them."

"Mom, we don't have much time," Wyatt said. "Those lizards are pulsating inside that mill—you should have seen them. They're going to break out into Baywood."

"What about the peacock feathers?" Julie asked. "Did you find them?"

Mrs. Sawyer nodded. "I did. But it's not what you're expecting." She opened the truck door and pulled a bag down from the front seat.

"What do you mean?" Wyatt asked.

"Here, Julie, you open it." Mrs. Sawyer handed her a plastic shopping bag.

Julie opened the top and looked into the bag. There were lots of peacock feathers, all right. She lifted one out, then realized the feathers had all been sewn together in some kind of . . . what?

"It's a costume. I forgot I had the feathers made into a headdress for a costume party," Mrs. Sawyer explained.

Julie lifted the headdress out. It wasn't just a headband with a few feathers decorating it; this was a full crown with strands of feathers and rhinestones hanging down.

"That's not all." Mrs. Sawyer nodded at the bag.

Julie looked deeper inside and pulled some clothing out. A feather-adorned black cloth emerged from the bag.

"That's a robe that went over my dress," Mrs. Sawyer said. "But on you, it will hang longer."

"You'll look like a real princess." Wyatt smiled.

"Or Big Bird." Julie frowned. "You think I should dress in that . . . costume and fight off the Skinks?"

Julie could feel her blood pounding. Would the Skinks crawl on her, trip her up, or end up in her hair? A chill raced from her scalp to her toes.

"Not fight them, exactly," Mrs. Sawyer said, looking apologetic. "Just scare them away from the back door toward the front exit."

"I'll have the van positioned at the front door. The back will be open, and the loading ramp will be down. They'll race inside, trying to escape. We'll shut them in with all that ice."

"Bye, bye lizards," Wyatt said.

"You really think it will work?" Julie asked.

"We'll have to go with it," Mrs. Sawyer said. She frowned. "Got to get rid of those lizardly things—whatever they are."

◇◇◇◇◇◇

Slizard peered through a crack above the front window of the grist mill. He'd heard a vehicle bumping down the slope of the hill.

The old grist mill had not been abandoned, after all. Someone remembered the path that led here. But why would they come?

A big van parked behind the tree as if in hiding. What were they planning?

A woman and two younger ones got out. A picnic?

Slizard's eyes bulged. It was Matt's Silvers's friend, Julie. And the two from the ice cream shop. They'd come for revenge.

Let them try. Glee rose up inside of him. The blue patches on his skin vibrated with excitement.

The Earples couldn't catch a Skink in a million years. Plus, the Skinks had creepy looks. Not great when attracting a mate, but handy when frightening the Earples.

The humans were scared. And Julie—the most squeamish of them all.

He'd form the Skinks into circles. If the three came into the mill, the Skinks would surround Julie. A good scream or two would send them all running for the truck. The town of Baywood would be open to attack.

Slizard would pay them back for delaying the plans of the Dark Void. He'd receive the highest honor from the Dweller.

Slizard pushed up on his legs. He'd be promoted to a higher rank—maybe even Ruler of the Rim!

⬡⬡⬡⬡⬡⬡

Mrs. Sawyer steered the truck as it backed downhill. She maneuvered over the plank bridge to the front porch. Wyatt jumped out, and Julie followed. He swung open the double doors on the back of the truck and lowered the ramp onto the porch.

Mrs. Sawyer nodded from the cab and gave a thumbs-up.

Wyatt jumped into the back of the van and brought out some ice blocks. Julie helped him stack the ice on each side of the ramp until they had a small wall. The Skinks wouldn't have a way around it.

Sweat beaded on Wyatt's forehead. He led Julie around to the side of the mill.

"Okay, Jules. I'm going to float ice in the channel around the water wheel so they won't jump out there. Then I'll go back to the front door and wait.

188

"When all the Skinks run into the van, I'll slam the doors shut and have them trapped. All we need now is for you to shoo them out—from inside the mill. Think you can handle it?"

Julie nodded.

Wyatt squeezed her hand and snuck around to the water wheel.

Julie's heart pounded. A side window was just above her head. She raised up on tiptoes and looked inside. The Skinks slithered around from every hole and crevice. She felt sick and ducked down.

○○○○○○

Slizard recruited the biggest and fastest Skink—Komo. He didn't have a handsome flaring collar like his own and wasn't nearly as clever. But he was strong and fast.

"So what's the plan, Slizard?" Komo raised up from his belly.

Slizard's tongue lashed out. "First, we scare the girl."

A face appeared in the window, then disappeared in a flash. The girl Julie was spying on them.

Oh, this will be good.

The Earples were closing in. Slizard had no doubt the Skinks could scare them off and disperse into town.

"The time is now," Slizard said. "Head to the back door. Scare the girl in every way you can. Run across her feet, circle her arms, and land on her head. She needs to scream loudly! Loud enough that the others who hear will back off!"

Komo wasted no time. He zipped to the back door, slithered up the frame, and wrapped his tail around a nail over the doorway. He'd dangle from above and drop into her hair.

Slizard and the rest of the Skinks waited in front of the back door. When she opened it, there'd be a big surprise.

○○○○○○

Julie let out a cleansing breath. Wasn't there some kind of wisdom for a situation like this?

Matt had told her that when he'd been trapped in the janitor's closet, he tried to think about all the good things instead of focusing on the bad. That had helped him not give in to fear until he'd found a way out.

Could she do the same?

She glanced into the bag. When Julie had first learned that she needed to find peacock feathers, she didn't have a clue where to find them. Yet here they were, as if by special delivery, just for her. That was a good thing.

And what about the ice water? Was it a coincidence that her new friend Wyatt and his family owned a shop with plenty of dry ice that wouldn't melt? How had *that* happened? Another thing in her favor.

Miss Duncan had revealed that Julie would have to step up and battle the Skinks. Had the Koinopian queen time-treaded to the future and somehow knew how this would play out? And had she known that Wyatt would arrive to help her?

Maybe.

But there was no doubt about it. This was Julie's time. She had to be brave.

Julie reached into the bag and brought out the headdress. She placed it on her head and adjusted it, then straightened the feathers and the strands of rhinestones that hung down the sides.

A smile touched her face. Just putting on the costume made her feel stronger. Wyatt had said she looked like a princess but she needed to be brave. More like a *Warrior Princess*!

The robe came next. Julie placed it around her shoulders and realized Mrs. Sawyer had been right. It covered almost to her feet. Feathers tickled her ankles.

Wyatt came back from the water wheel. "Everything's set. I put so much ice in that water it's almost like a slushie." Then, "Ready to go in? The back door's only a few steps around the corner."

Julie stood tall and lifted her head. Her eyes stared ahead. She hoped she looked as tough as a Sphinx in the Egyptian desert. She breathed out, steadying herself for what would come next.

"I'm ready."

Chapter Twenty-Seven

WARRIOR PRINCESS

Julie braced herself and walked to the back door. Multitudes of Skinks waited on the other side. She'd glimpsed them through the window as they'd slithered around. Would the peacock feathers work?

She had to trust that Miss Duncan knew the ways of Koinopia and how to battle the slimy creatures who'd emerged from the Dark Void.

Julie placed her hand on the doorknob and turned it. The old door squeaked as it opened into the large room.

Skinks moved around in a mass, a huge quivering wave that might break and roll in her direction at any moment.

She started to step in, then—

The ugliest, biggest, green-humped creature she'd ever seen dangled from its tail in front of the doorway. She didn't scream; she knew she had to be strong.

Then, the strangest thing. The creature's green pebbly skin paled and its eyes widened. The long tail shortened and retracted the Skink back up to wherever it had dangled from. Where did it go?

Had it been afraid? *Of her*?

Julie sneezed. The dusty feathers did have a smell—the odor of a peacock. The hated enemy of every lizard or lizard-like creature in existence.

She took a step inside.

⬡⬡⬡⬡⬡⬡

Slizard pumped up on his legs and saw Komo dangling in front of the door opening. Julie had dared to open the door!

Ah! Matt Silvers and his friends would soon know the frightening power of the Skinks! Oh, how they'd creep and slither and slide around the girl!

Late afternoon light seeped into the room. An exotic smell rushed in from outside.

Slime dripped from Komo as he swung up and away from the door opening. *What* was he doing?

Komo froze above the door, then crept down the wall and back into the mass of Skinks that crowded the room.

Slizard sniffed the air. It couldn't be. The smell. The stink of their arch enemy filled the room and it was overpowering.

He dared to look up. There stood the tallest, most hideous creature he'd ever glimpsed. The emerald feathers had huge, dark eyes that momentarily paralyzed Slizard. He'd seen the feathers before on their most fearsome adversaries—peacocks that watched a Skink's every move, snapped them up with sharp beaks, and swallowed them whole in one gulp.

But this peacock had a face. Had Julie tricked them into believing she was an Earple when she was actually this *thing*?

The peacock creature moved into the room, feathers swaying, arms flapping, and legs striding forward.

Blood surged into Slizard's limbs, and he could finally move. He had to get away from the feathers and the smell. He joined the mound of Skinks that now gathered in the center of the room. They'd smelled the odor of the enemy.

The Skinks climbed over one another and slithered away from *the thing* toward the front door. Some disappeared behind the large stone and onto the big wheel. Anywhere to escape!

✦✦✦✦✦✦

Julie entered the mill through the back door. No doubt about it. The Skinks were afraid—of her! They ran and squirmed in every direction, froze, then wriggled away as fast as they could.

She waved her arms, and the Skinks surged away from her toward the front door. The humped lizards erupted from under loose boards, old bags of meal, and hidden nests. With her every step, they darted further away in a panic.

Her robe whirled around her as she turned in one direction and then the other, scaring them with a swirl of her black, feathered cloak.

Julie's determined jaw relaxed, and a smile touched the corners of her mouth. This whole scene, creepy and surreal, started to be fun.

Julie Spencer—the *Warrior Princess*—would chase her evil enemies to their ruin, banishing them forever to a frozen dungeon!

A few Skinks jumped into the water around the water wheel. But no worries. Wyatt's ice bath would freeze them like lizardy popsicles.

The front door of the mill creaked open and the Skinks saw an escape. In a frenzy, they streamed out of the mill and onto the porch. Behind them, Julie swirled and fanned her arms until they crowded out the front entrance. They darted to the ice wall, then turned and ran up the dark ramp into the icy bed of the Creamy Cone truck.

Julie moved to the front porch just in time to see Wyatt slam the double doors shut, trapping the Skinks inside.

"You've done it!" Julie cried.

Wyatt smiled wide. "No, *we've* done it. I knew you had it in you. Way to go, princess!"

"That's *Warrior Princess*, if you don't mind," Julie laughed. Relief and happiness flowed through her. She jokingly punched his shoulder.

Wyatt hugged her. Her heart beat a little faster, and she wondered. *Was he just celebrating, or was it something else?*

They'd beat the Dark Void again! The Skinks were trapped and paralyzed, no longer a threat to the town of Baywood.

⬡⬡⬡⬡⬡⬡

"Hey, you two! Did it work?" Wyatt's mother called out the truck window.

"Yeah, stellar!" Wyatt said. "I think we got them all."

Mrs. Sawyer pulled the truck to the top of the hill and stopped. The driver's side door opened, and she jumped out. "I'll help you make sure!"

As she walked toward them, C.C. started rolling backward.

"Mom! Did you set the parking brake?" Wyatt yelled.

"Oh no!" Julie cried.

The Creamy Cone van picked up speed as it rolled down the hill toward the river.

"The brake! It's not working!" Mrs. Sawyer yelled.

Wyatt took off as if he could catch the van, and Julie ran after him. The dent on the side of the truck was leaking fluid.

The truck headed toward the creek. The under-body of the truck screeched as it crashed over a tree stump next to the water.

Boom!

A spark ignited, and flames shot up.

The back tires of the van rolled into the water. Liquid flowed out the side, and Julie smelled gas. Black smoke boiled out.

"Julie, Wyatt! Get back!" Mrs. Sawyer ordered.

Wyatt pulled Julie hard, back up the hill.

ROAR!

The truck exploded behind them.

Julie turned. Parts of the Creamy Cone truck—tires, bolts, and part of a door—blasted high into the sky.

She ran with Wyatt behind the mill and waited until the explosions stopped and the roar quieted. The air smelled like burnt rubber, and black smoke billowed up from the water.

"Wonder if the Skinks escaped?" Julie worried.

"I'm pretty sure they're toasted," Wyatt said.

She peered around the corner of the mill. "The gas has leaked into the creek. The water is burning!"

Julie walked carefully, until she stood halfway down the hill. She squinted to see closer.

A few Skinks were streaming out of the van's bent back doors.

Oh no! *Can't they be killed?*

The humped creatures crept and maneuvered sideways across the metal panels of the truck as if they were dizzy. And they weren't coming back up the hill. Instead, they headed for the circle of flaming water and dove in.

Julie glanced into the evening twilight. The moon started to rise in the East.

A full moon and fire on the water. That's how the Skinks had arrived in Baywood. They were returning the same way!

The Skinks dropped into the water, disappearing into the boggy depths. She ran to the water's edge. A whirlpool turned within the ring of fire, and the Skinks descended into the whirling waves, green humps and lizardy tails swirling until they disappeared.

She hoped they'd been swallowed up by the Dark Void.

Never to return.

FLASH AND A CLASH

Wrinkles raced through the Rim as fast as his wrinkly body would carry him. Matt's dog seemed to know instinctively he'd been called upon to save the day—like this was his one chance to prove he could do more than trot around the house and run after the balls Grandpa threw him.

And it wouldn't be the first time Wrinkles had helped Matt on his quest for the rubies. Matt had found the third ruby on Wrinkle's sparkly collar. Maybe his dog remembered Jasper. After all, he'd been Jasper's courier.

Black dust swirled up around them—Wrinkles, plus the two horses, stirred up the sandy sentiment of the Rim into a cloud. Matt continually checked on Ryan, who'd nearly slipped off of Wrinkles a couple of times.

Matt coughed. "Are we getting close to where you spied the Wolvin gathering?"

Noris nodded. "Aye, but we have searched all around that rocky enclave. We found no trace of Bounded Hollow."

Wrinkles continued further, and started panting. The horses, too, needed a break.

"We've got to find water," Matt said.

"I remember a stream just ahead," Juman lifted his chin.

Wrinkles slowed to a trot, and the horses passed him. Matt followed his two Valenian friends as they guided their horses to the water. The desert-like surroundings gave way to a small island of grass.

"There's water, boy." Matt patted Wrinkles. Wrinkles walked forward to the stream.

Matt tapped Ryan's knee. "Ryan!"

"Huh?"

"We've got to slide down. There's water."

Ryan nodded. Matt slid down Wrinkles' leg first, and Ryan followed. Wrinkles moved closer to the water and lowered his head for a drink.

"I still feel kind of sick," Ryan said. He splashed water on his face.

"You need something to drink with, young friends?" Juman offered his metal cup to Ryan.

Ryan took a long drink with the cup and passed it to Matt.

Noris came over. "Are we any closer, Matthew?"

Matt shrugged. Wrinkles had finished drinking and moved a few yards away from them. He paced back and forth next to the stream.

"That hound is restless," Noris said.

Wrinkles barked, then jumped, causing the ground to shake. He rotated in a circle as if he were frustrated.

"Hey, Wrinkles!" Matt called. Wrinkles looked up, then began scratching with his front claws.

"Is he looking for food?" Juman asked. "Perhaps a mole is under there."

"I don't think so," Matt answered.

"Juman," Noris began. "What is it Adren had said about Bounded Hollow?"

"That the Wolvin there are especially vicious?" Juman answered. Matt shuddered.

"No," Noris said. "Something else—it is a cave."

Matt studied Wrinkles. "Boy, calm down."

Wrinkles quit jumping but paced next to the stream.

And then, as if a clear light had penetrated the dim glow of the Rim, Matt suddenly knew where they would find Jasper.

"The cave is below us."

○○○○○○

One of the Wolvin, who'd entered the prison chamber with Fury, sat before Jasper. The creature tilted its head.

"This one is aged. He might be tough, but chewy." A tongue glided across its mouth. "Like jerky." He nipped Jasper's hand.

Anger flared in Jasper's being. If only he had his sword . . . his armor . . . his strength. To be captured while in a human covering had brought him a weakness he had never experienced.

Human bodies were mortal and passing away. And yet the Eternal One cared so much for them. A mystery indeed.

Above them, the ground shook. A piece of rock dislodged from the ceiling and fell, cracking against the hard bottom of their chamber. Another rumble, and pieces of stone fell all around him. Dust showered down from the ceiling. An earthquake?

The rumbling stopped, but a large rock had fallen within Jasper's grasp. The Wolvin hadn't noticed.

Fury searched the ceiling. "We don't have much time. This chamber could cave in." He paced in front of Jasper. "Unchain him from the wall, Sizor. We will parade him through the cavern for all to see before delivering him to the fire."

"There is a neck ring," Devon crouched and padded to a shadowed area of the chamber. He stood and lifted a large shackle from the wall. He grasped it with his webbed toes and brought it to Fury.

Fury raised the neck shackle above Jasper's head.

"No!" Petrus cried weakly. "You cannot! Have you no fear of the mighty Guardian?"

"Not so mighty now!" Fury growled. The other Wolvin howled.

Fury dropped the iron neck ring over Jasper's head. Jasper turned his neck side-to-side in protest, but it was no use. The ring settled just above his shoulders. Fury attached a long chain.

"You will not escape punishment for this, Fury!" Petrus croaked, his eyes moist.

Jasper pulled against the ring, but it dug into his skin and made him dizzy. Devon and Sizor lifted him up to stand.

Jasper wavered under the heavy iron of the loose chains and shackles. He fell back, but the two Wolvin caught him.

"Shall we march?" Devon asked.

"Into the passageway, so the other prisoners may see what awaits them," Fury's yellow eyes gleamed.

"And what about the dainty prince?" Devon bared his fangs.

"He will be next." Fury glanced at Petrus. "Do not forget the Guardian's cape!" he growled, jerking the cape away from Petrus's shoulders, and draping it over Jasper.

"All hail the mighty Guardian!" Fury shouted.

The three howled and jeered. Petrus stared, his eyes burning with anguish.

Footsteps echoed into the chamber from the dark corridor.

"Others are coming to join us?" Sizor peered into the dark passageway.

"They have heard our victory cries!" Fury nodded. "They have come to witness the humiliation!"

"I thought they waited at the bonfire?" Sizor's dark eyes drew together.

A blinding light flashed into the chamber. The Wolvin hid their faces. Petrus bowed his head.

Jasper's weak legs surged with new strength. Was it possible? Could it be?

Matt Silvers entered their chamber, two orbs held high in his hands! The young Valenian's determined face was set like stone as he marched into the den of their capture.

"Jasper!" Matt cried. "I have the Stones of Fire!"

The power of the Stones bathed their chamber in fiery light.

"Matt, you have come!" Jasper shouted.

Noris flew in behind Matt and knelt beside Petrus. "My prince! What have they done to you?"

Noris raised his sword and brought it down on Petrus's chains. The chains clanged but did not release him. Through squinting eyes, Devon bared his claws and swiped at Noris. The claws penetrated Noris's fur mantle, and blood surged out. He attacked Devon with his sword, cutting deeply into the Wolvin's hand and arm.

"*AAR!* What have you done?" Devon howled in pain and scampered out of the room.

"*Woff, Wooo!*" Fury ignited. He jerked the chain around Jasper's neck.

The fiery light of the Stones strengthened Jasper and he yanked back, slinging Fury through the air. The Wolvin crashed against the wall and fell to the floor. He lay still on the cold stone.

Sizor crouched behind Juman's back. Jasper grasped the rock beside him and hurled it at Sizor as he flew at Juman with open jaws. The stone struck the Wolvin's ear, knocking his head to the side. Sizor's howl of pain caused Juman to turn. He struck the Wolvin with his mace and Sizor collapsed to the ground.

Matt wasted no time. He touched Jasper's shackles with the Stones of Fire, and in one bright streaming flame, the iron cuffs and chains disintegrated into dust.

Joy overwhelmed Jasper. "Praise be to the Eternal One!"

Petrus stood up next to the wall. Noris's sword strike hadn't freed him. Now, his face brightened with hope.

Matt hurried to Petrus's side and touched the Stones to his shackles. The fire shot forth from the Stones, but not as strong as before. Petrus's cuffs diminished but still encircled his wrists.

"Jasper, what has happened? The Stones of Fire haven't released him!" Matt's face crumpled in distress. He handed the Stones to Jasper as if he could make them work.

Jasper examined the Stones, one in each hand. Alarm rose in his heart.

"The power of these Stones has diminished. It is many centuries since they were ignited in Koinopia." His heart thumped against his chest as he hid the fading Stones in the pocket of his cloak. "You found only two Stones among the Druids?"

"That's all!" Matt shouted, panic rising in his voice. "I didn't see any others!"

Petrus glanced down at his swollen wrists.

Matt bowed his head in a prayer. When he raised his head, Jasper saw the answer.

"Matt, what is that around your neck?"

Matt's hand went to the leather strand and the white stone that hung from it. His eyes widened. "This stone the Valenians gave me . . . it is a Stone of Fire?"

"Yes, young Valenian!" Petrus raised his head.

Jasper nodded. "Hewn from the very same mountain in Koinopia!"

Relief and excitement flowed among the companions of light.

Matt untied the leather necklace from his neck. The white stone became clear, and a small fire inside flared up and filled the orb. Matt touched the stone to Petrus's chains, and a stream of light burst forth, turning the iron links and shackles to dust.

Petrus rubbed his wrists, then held his arms high. "All thanks to the Eternal One! You have rescued us, young Valenian!"

Chapter Twenty-Nine

INTO THE LIGHT

Fury lay silent on the floor of the prison chamber. The torch he had dropped burned, filling the chamber with smoke. Matt coughed. Flaming pitch permeated the room, and his eyes stung. He picked up the torch and started out of the den.

"Let's get out of here! The other Wolvin might come back."

"Aye!" Noris answered. "They are still gathered at the bonfire. Make haste before they return!"

Behind Matt, Noris supported Petrus, his arm flung around Noris's strong neck. Juman steadied Jasper as they walked side by side.

Matt held the torch in front as he strode forward. To his right, a chamber appeared in the flickering light.

"The others," Jasper spoke from behind him. "We must set them free."

Matt stopped and pushed on a door fashioned of tree limbs, the branches tightened together with rope.

"It's not budging." He held the torch to the rope, and the fibers singed and burned away. The branches fell to the cavern floor.

Two captives appeared in the opening—an older woman in rags held a young girl.

"Oh, thank the Eternal One. We are free!" the woman shouted.

"Come, quickly!" Juman urged.

The woman hurried out of her chamber, clutching the girl in her arms.

"Are there others?" Jasper asked.

"There is another chamber," the woman said. A large room where men are bound."

Matt hurried ahead to the next chamber. Juman crashed his mace against the door, and it crumbled. Inside the larger room, at least twenty men, frail and whiskered, stood staring at the opening.

"We heard the uproar!" an older man shouted.

"I dared to hope for rescue!" a younger man cried as he hurried toward the chamber opening. "We are free! The Eternal One be praised!" He bounded out of the cell into the corridor. The other men hurried after him, fleeing from the chamber.

"Quickly now!" Juman urged them as they surrounded him and Jasper.

Matt led them all, surging ahead. The wet cavern floor slowed his ascent up the narrow, dark steps. Finally, the corridor lightened, and just ahead, the gleaming sun guided them up and out of the dark cavern.

They were free!

Matt squinted into the sunlight. To his right, Ryan sat atop Wrinkles.

"Matt! Get up here!" Ryan shouted. "The Wolvin are just over the next hill!"

"Go ahead, young Silvers!" Noris shouted. "We will guide the others to our hideout. But you must return home!"

Wrinkles lowered, and Matt skimmed up onto his back.

"But I don't know the way home from here!" Matt slid under Wrinkles's collar and held on.

Jasper spoke up. "Find the Prism Bridge. From there, you may cross into Koinopia."

"Will you come with us?" Matt pleaded.

Jasper looked up and down, taking in Wrinkles. He looked doubtful.

"Mighty Guardian, you may have my horse," Juman offered. "In my sack are rations—honey and bread, a side of jerky, a skin of water."

Jasper nodded. "Your generosity will not be forgotten."

Juman helped Jasper onto the saddle. Noris settled Petrus on his horse and prepared to walk beside him.

"I bid you farewell, mighty Guardian!" Petrus croaked. "We are brothers forever."

Jasper raised his right hand in salute. "Forever."

"Be off, young Valenian!" Noris called to Matt. "It—has been an honor." He bowed his head, then quickened his steps as he and Juman led Petrus and the freed prisoners away toward the Valenian camp.

◇◇◇◇◇◇

From on top of Wrinkles, Matt peered down at Jasper as he trotted beside them on Juman's horse.

"Is it almost nighttime here?" Matt asked. The light of the Rim had grown dimmer, even though Matt could still see around him. In the distance near the Glops, lightning streaked through the sky.

Jasper glanced up. "Yes. We need to find shelter."

"But where?" Matt asked. The desert plain of the Rim had given way to short trees and Prickleberry bushes in the Glops.

Jasper searched the horizon. "There is no more fire near the Woodlands." He peered closer, and a smile lit his face. "The Valenians have fought and turned back the enemy!"

"But Petrus—their prince—was in prison!" Matt said.

Jasper nodded. "But they continued to fight!" He raised a fist in victory.

"I'm glad the smoke is gone," Ryan said. It's the first thing I remember after getting zapped here." His smile faded. "Sure want to get back home."

"You are worried about returning home?" Jasper's voice had gained strength since he'd eaten Juman's provisions.

"My parents think I'm at basketball camp." Ryan, too, seemed more like himself. "I've been gone a week. If I'm not back by Sunday night, Mom will be hoppin'."

"It was Sunday after lunch when I left," Matt said.

Ryan shook his head. "Man! I'll never make it. The whole police department will be out looking for me." He called down to Jasper. "Can you reach out to Queen Anne? Or should I say, 'Miss Duncan,' And ask her what time it is at home?"

Jasper glanced up. "An excellent idea. Now to find a quiet place where there are no distractions. My voice will be even stronger there. You two remain here."

Jasper turned his horse and rode off toward the border of the Woodlands. The trees untouched by the fire stood tall, and the grass grew green and lush. Queen Anne might hear Jasper more clearly in that quiet place—away from the horses neighing and the cracks of lightning.

Wrinkles slowed to a stop and lowered. Matt and Ryan slid down.

"We better look for a place to hide out," Ryan said.

"Yeah?" Matt searched around.

"The storms in the Glops? They're scary. Big time," Ryan said.

A munching sound came from behind one of the stubby trees.

"Ryan, you hear that?" Matt tilted his head toward the sound. "I know the spongy swamp is near here. Do they have alligators?"

"No, it's too boring for that."

Matt saw movement behind one of the bushes. "There's something over there."

A pale head appeared.

"Dude, come out! We see you," Ryan called.

A creature came from behind the bush and moved like an otter over the soft ground.

"Dawdle?" Ryan's eyes grew wide.

"I think you remember me," Dawdle said.

Matt turned. "So this is your friend?"

Ryan nodded. "That's him."

Wrinkles chuffed behind them, scaring Dawdle. He hid behind a bush.

"It's okay," Matt said. "My dog won't hurt you."

A few moments passed, and Dawdle slid forward. "It might be that I wish to travel with you."

"For real?" Ryan asked.

"Your visit might have changed me."

"But how?"

"That spark," Dawdle said quietly. "The spark in your eyes when you spoke of Koinopia."

"Wait, you're *sure* about that?" Ryan laughed. "You don't mean it *might* have been the spark?"

Dawdle's pale cheeks reddened. "Yes, I am sure." His whiskers bristled. "For the first time in a long while."

Matt nudged Ryan. "No one ever complimented me on having a 'spark.'"

Ryan smiled a little, but Dawdle's eyes glistened.

"What's up, Dawdle?" Ryan asked.

"It is just that—" He looked past them as if searching for the right words. "I once felt that joy, that light that shone in your face when you spoke of Koinopia." He looked down. "But I lost it. I had forgotten why I started the journey to Koinopia to begin with."

Matt and Ryan exchanged glances.

"It's never too late to begin again," Matt said.

"We have a Guardian who knows the way," Ryan added. "He is taking us to the Prism Bridge."

"The Prism Bridge!" Dawdle's nose twitched.

"And into Koinopia," Matt said.

"Yes, please, may I go with you?"

Matt thought he saw a spark in Dawdle's eyes.

"Can you follow behind us?" Matt asked. There was no more room atop Wrinkles.

Soft clopping came from the short trees in front of them. Jasper appeared, his cloak covering his thin frame. His face still looked pale, but he'd regained his stately bearing. "The small creature can ride with me," Jasper said. "There is room in Juman's bag, I believe."

"I think this is the greatest thing I could hope for!" Dawdle bristled and slid over to Jasper. "To finally arrive in Koinopia and with this wise Guardian!"

"You *think* this is the greatest thing?" Ryan asked.

Dawdle's brown eyes swiveled to Ryan. "No, my Earple friend. I am no longer doubting. I am sure."

Dawdle's whiskers twitched as he gazed up at Jasper. Dawdle stood on his hind legs, and one paw went to his mouth. "How should I climb up?"

"No worries," Ryan said. He moved to Jasper's side, lifted the flap of Juman's bag, and placed Dawdle inside. Dawdle pumped his legs and spun around—furry bottom, head, forelegs, tail—until he finally settled his body in the bag. His head remained visible above, and his front paws hung over the side.

"Are we ready?" Jasper had watched the whole wriggling episode. His eyes twinkled. Was he smiling?

A lightning flash crackled in the sky, closer to them. Darkness had settled in the Glops.

"The storm gets closer. Where do we hide out?" Matt climbed to his place atop Wrinkles and Ryan joined him.

"We do not hide," Jasper said. "I have discovered it is not far to the Prism Bridge and the Woodland Border from here. We will travel there and escape the storm."

"But Jasper, what about Queen Anne? Did you contact her?" Ryan asked.

Jasper nodded. "You have exactly one hour, in Earth time, to return."

Ryan closed his eyes. "I'm doomed."

"We have no time to waste." Jasper's heels nudged the horse, and they shot toward the remaining light shining over the trees in the Woodlands.

Matt patted Wrinkles's head. "Let's go!"

THE PRISM BRIDGE

Matt and Ryan hung on as Wrinkles galloped toward the light. Ahead of them, Jasper guided Juman's horse, Banner, to the edge of the Rim, where the swampy surroundings gave way to grassland. Strangely, the darkness of the Rim did not overtake them as they came closer to Koinopia. The lightning, too, had dissipated. Instead of darker night, the day grew brighter.

Dawdle seemed to survey the changing landscape with wonder. "I had forgotten this," Dawdle said. Then, "Oh, the grass! And there are real trees in the distance!"

They topped a hill, and Jasper pulled on Banner's reins, halting the horse. Wrinkles stopped beside them.

Jasper glanced up at Matt and Ryan. "We rest here." Below them, a river flowed.

"Now?" Ryan asked. "But we're so close. I have to make it home on time!"

"There is a perfect time for everything," Jasper said.

Matt turned to Ryan. "What's the worse thing that can happen?"

"Zillions of things." Ryan shook his head. "Coach returns, and I'm not with him. Mom and Dad panic; the police are called. The whole town thinks I've been kidnapped. Parents lock up their kids, thinking someone might take them." Ryan sighed. "No one will trust anyone.

"Plus, they'll want us to explain where I've been for a week. And what about the Skinks? Wonder if they've taken over?"

Matt had to admit he had the same fears. If he didn't return Sunday night, his own family would panic. And he'd worried about Julie, fighting off the Skinks alone.

On Sunday afternoon, Matt had told his mother he was going to search for Wrinkles. That seemed like eons ago!

"We must rest and prepare." Jasper dismounted and led Banner to the streaming river.

Wrinkles followed and lowered to let Matt and Ryan slide down. They all drank. Matt hadn't realized how thirsty he'd become.

Silvery notes resounded around the hills, filling Matt with wonder. He lifted his eyes from the stream.

"Is that music I hear?" Matt asked.

"Yes, the Koinopian trumpets are drawing you forward." Jasper nodded.

Above the next hill, a different kind of light hovered. The atmosphere shimmered like waves of heat on a summer day. Only these waves had color, and they were very clear—not hazy.

"And that light, is it coming from the Prism Bridge?"

"Yes. It is the reason I stopped," Jasper said. "To prepare before we move on."

"So, how do we get ready?" Matt asked.

"We will walk through the stream to the other bank."

"Whoa." Matt's eye twitched. He didn't want to get wet, and there was no telling how deep the water was. But the black dust of the Rim clung to him. It would feel good to get rid of the scratchy sand.

"For real?" Ryan asked. "Walking through water? But I'm not that dirty."

"Ryan, look at your shoes," Matt said.

The pink, spongy stuff from the Glops was stuck to Ryan's shoes. They were also on his jeans. He frowned and brushed at the sticky glop.

"What about you, Jasper?" Matt asked.

"You have no idea how I have longed for a bath. To wash away the filth of these prison clothes."

"But where is your armor? And the mantle you sometimes wore?" Matt asked.

"When I visited you at home that last day, I had only my cloak and the clothes worn by Earples," Jasper said. "That is how the Wolvin captured me."

Matt nodded. Then, "What about Wrinkles? Can he cross over?"

"And don't forget me!" Dawdle said.

Banner whinnied.

"The others may follow us across," Jasper said. "I will lead you."

Jasper stepped into the stream and Matt followed.

The cool water rushed over Matt's shoes and he hopped. His feet tingled, but he kept moving forward until the stream reached his knees.

"What temperature is this? Zero?" Ryan said as he followed, hip-hopping.

Dawdle paddled into the stream and turned onto his back. "Oh, I could get used to this."

Water splashed and sloshed. Banner's legs pumped up and down as he moved through the shallow stream.

Wrinkles jumped in next, causing a wave to splash over Matt's head, drenching his hair.

As the water got deeper, the soft bottom of the stream fell away, and Matt floated through the deep middle. He thought he might have to swim, but the stream carried him along and he floated to the other shore.

Jasper emerged from the stream first, water dripping from his clothes as he stepped out of the shallow water onto the bank. His cloak, once smudged black by the burning torches of the prison, now glistened white. His body looked restored and powerful—his former Koinopian form.

Now in shallow water, Matt's feet sank into the soft soil. He splashed through the clear water to the bank. He no longer felt the grit of the Rim, and his own clothes looked brand-new.

Ryan splashed behind him. He looked super clean, and the gloppy stuff had come from his shoes and pants.

Dawdle's head peeked up from the water, and it was no longer bare but covered in thick, brown fur. His abundant whiskers bristled, and he now had eyebrows. He stood in the water and glanced down at his forelegs.

"I've got my fur back! I'm no longer naked!"

Ryan laughed. Matt and Jasper joined him.

"Dawdle, you may swim through the river—follow it and cross into Koinopia," Jasper told him. "We will see you on the other side!"

Dawdle's head bobbed, then he dove back into the deep waves of the river and followed it toward Koinopia.

Banner's hooves printed the wet sand as he emerged from the water. His mighty neck swung side-to-side and water flew from his mane. Banner snorted, his ears pointing forward and his tail raised high as he raced onto shore. From his strong sides, wings emerged and flapped, lifting him into the air. His front legs curved under him, and his back hooves flew behind him as he tilted upward.

"Banner!" Jasper shouted. "We thank you for your help."

A strong whinny resounded from Banner's muzzle.

"Now return to Juman and the Valenian camp! They need you!" Jasper called.

Banner turned around and lifted above their heads, his head held high. He soared, his wings carrying him back over the hill toward the Rim and his Valenian master, Juman.

"Wow!" Matt's head jerked back.

"Dude's riding the wind!" Ryan craned his neck, tracing Banner's flight.

Matt searched the river. "Wait, where's Wrinkles?"

He'd gotten used to easily spotting his enormous dog, but he didn't see him anywhere.

A yip, then a bark came from downstream. Matt turned. Wrinkles came running toward him, only he wasn't huge! His best dog had come back to him—his regular size! Matt squatted down, and Wrinkles ran into his arms.

"There, boy!" He'd missed being able to give him a real hug.

Ryan came over. "What's up, Wrinkles? He smoothed his head as Matt held him.

"Reunions make me happy," Jasper said. "But time is passing here. We can not linger."

Matt remembered his watch. The face glowed. The watch began working, and zoomed forward until it showed one minute before six o'clock.

"Ryan! Quick! We've got to make it over the hill to the Prism Bridge. There's just one minute left before time runs out!"

"But we still won't be home, will we?"

"No, but remember? Time stands still in Koinopia! We have to cross over!"

"Hurry now!" Jasper grunted up the hill ahead of them. Matt could tell Jasper's full strength hadn't yet returned.

Matt knew he could make it to the top—he and Ryan were the fastest players on the basketball team. He ran hard, but halfway up, his legs ached and he panted. This last hill to the Prism Bridge seemed straight up.

Ryan ran beside him, pumping his arms and panting. "Let's go!" He linked arms with Matt and helped him tread up the toughest part of the hill.

Wrinkles barked at Matt's heels, and he dug in harder until he and Ryan ran side-by-side. Jasper crested the hill. He stood tall, waiting for them.

The top of the hill drew nearer with every stride. Matt finally reached the high point with Ryan's help.

Matt gasped.

A beautiful valley opened before them. Gemstones of every color glowed like clear, jeweled bricks paving a road and leading to a triple-arched bridge. Rubies and sapphires, emeralds and diamonds, and the rest—he couldn't name all the jewels, curved above the bridge in a span of myriad colors.

Pure white light shone through the gemstones like a prism, releasing hues Matt had never seen before. Deep and vibrant. So filled with energy that the colors seemed to pulse with life.

"Whoa." Matt didn't have the words.

"Intense," Ryan said.

Jasper stood still, but his words carried urgency. "Hurry over now, before Earth-time runs out!"

Matt and Ryan flew down the slope and glided over the gemstone bricks. White light danced along Ryan's back in rippling waves. The waves embraced Matt's body, and the light danced over them and between them, as brilliant as blinding snow but with every color of the universe.

They entered the bridge. Were they riding a lightning bolt? Every cell in Matt's body ignited with strength. On they soared, their feet barely touching the golden-glass pavement. They passed under the first jeweled arch, rainbow light drenching them. The second and third arches bathed them in twinkling color. Time collapsed into one eternal moment as they crossed the bridge and emerged on the other side, safely in Koinopia.

Jasper arrived behind them, his cloak now glistening and flowing, his emerald eyes ignited with new life. A meadow opened before them, and the flowers bowed their blossoming heads as Jasper passed by.

"Ah, how blessed it is to be at home!" Jasper's voice echoed through the flowers and grass, bending them. He turned in a circle, hands raised as if in greeting. His lips pursed and he released a whistle, loud and long.

The meadow stilled in silence, then hoofbeats resounded over the hills and grew louder, like heavy raindrops on a windowpane. A golden head bobbed through the meadow, then a strong chest, legs, and hooves became visible. A tail flowed behind the galloping horse, whisked by the wind. Jasper's golden steed pranced to where they stood.

"Torch!" Jasper called.

Torch raised his head and snorted. His tail flowed behind him, and Jasper smoothed his neck as he greeted him.

"So good to see you, my friend!" Jasper rubbed Torch's back.

"I guess we know how you're getting home," Ryan said.

"Oh, but not to despair, young man!" Jasper gazed at Ryan as he continued to inspect Torch's reins and saddle.

"What do we do now?" Matt said. "The red chest is at the Crystal Cavern. It's our only way back."

"What did I tell you when I left Baywood, after we'd defeated the Craevin?" Jasper asked.

The last month scrolled through Matt's brain. He remembered the day after they'd defeated the Craevin. They'd sat in his mother's flower garden early that Sunday morning, basking in the victory. Then, Jasper had disappeared, but his words remained behind.

You will not walk alone.

"You're telling me I'm not alone, right?"

"Yes, and that you always have help," Jasper said. "Even now, when you need to return home."

To his left, a rock outcropping bordered a stream. Matt walked over and sat on the cool stone. Ryan followed, and Jasper led Torch over for a drink.

"I've had lots of help," Matt said. "Miss Duncan, to begin with—who is also Queen Anne. She let us know you were in trouble."

"And Julie's been fighting the Skinks in Baywood," Ryan reminded him. "Until we get back."

"Yeah," Matt said.

"How did you find the Stones of Fire?" Jasper asked.

"Dad had a trip to Scotland. And Stubley appeared—as a chauffeur—to hurry me along. Then, there was Mr. Bridges on the train. He told us about the Druids in Scotland and where I might find them. But he also gave me a warning."

"So, help and a warning at the same time?" Jasper asked.

"Yeah, I guess that's right."

"And we had this driver at St. Andrews, who told us about the churches and cemeteries in Scotland but also warned me about the Druid gatherings."

"So help and a warning again?" Jasper nodded.

Matt nodded. "Bruce also rescued me in the woods. And so did lightning quickness and beyond-seeing."

"Gifts from the Valenians, I believe." Jasper crossed his arms.

"Zow, all that happened?" Ryan asked. "While I slept five days at the Glops! I hope I never waste time like that again."

"Did anyone else help?"

Matt nodded. "I thought I'd lost the Stones of Fire. The Druids followed me to Loch Ness and stole my backpack. I jumped into a deep lake, thinking I could swim and catch them. How bonehead was that?"

"Cringey," Ryan said.

A smile crossed Jasper's face. "And what kept you from drowning?"

"I don't exactly know," Matt said. " A creature of some kind. Pushed me up from the bottom."

"Wha?" Ryan's mouth dropped open. "You don't mean—The Loch Ness *monster*?"

Matt shrugged. "Not sure, but it had a big snout. And the lake bubbled."

"No way!" Ryan said.

"Are you forgetting anyone?" Jasper asked.

"Mom and Dad," Matt answered, nodding.

"Mom went with me to Dunino and drove me back from the Druid's den. And she didn't know it, but she kept the Stones of Fire from being stolen by Balmore."

"We often do things without knowing they are for our good. Or for someone else's," Jasper said.

"At Loch Ness, Dad pulled me out of the lake and wrapped me in a blanket," Matt added.

"As did the boat captain?" Jasper asked.

"Him, too." Matt sighed. "I guess there were a lot of people helping me."

"Not all Earples," Jasper said.

"Yeah," Matt said. He hadn't realized it until Jasper reminded him. "Wrinkles, Noris, Juman, Banner, and Vagabond."

"And?"

Matt glanced beside him at Ryan. "There was one more person. Ryan pulled me to the top of that last hill."

"So now you realize—you are not alone," Jasper said.

"And neither were you, Jasper," Ryan spoke up.

"It is truth," Jasper nodded. "I thank the Eternal One for sending you to rescue me and keeping you safe."

Torch neighed.

"And for your own courage and bravery." Jasper knelt on one knee and bowed his head.

"You are the one who suffered in that prison," Matt said. He felt uncomfortable that his mentor and Guardian had humbled himself.

"And now I am home again," Jasper smiled and stood. "And I have something for you." He reached into Torch's saddle bag and brought out the red chest.

"Torch brought this from the Crystal Cavern!"

"Yes." Jasper handed the chest to Matt. "And perhaps you should open it."

Matt cradled the chest in one arm and opened it. Inside rested a rolled-up scroll with a red ribbon tied around it.

"The message of the sixth ruby!" Matt had been so intent on finding Jasper that he hadn't looked for another message.

"Yes," Jasper said. "You have accomplished much, young Valenian. By finding the Stones of Fire and rescuing me, you have made great strides. Yet your training must continue."

Matt set the chest on the rock beside him, and the lid softly closed. He unrolled the paper.

Where your treasure is, there will your heart be also.

He glanced up at Jasper. "My treasure? Like the Stones of Fire?"

Jasper nodded. "Those could be counted among your treasures, yes. In seeking them, you have strengthened your faith."

Something occurred to Matt. He'd given the Stones of Fire to Jasper during the rescue at Bounded Hollow.

"Do you still have the Stones?" Matt asked.

"They are among the things you treasure?" Jasper brought the Stones out from his cloak and held them in his open hand.

"Yes. But would you keep them safe for me here?"

Jasper nodded and studied him. "If your treasure is here, does that mean your heart is here also?"

"Koinopia is important to me," Matt said.

"Then you have fulfilled the message of the sixth ruby." Jasper bowed his head slightly.

"That one was easy," Matt smiled. His tone softened. "But I'm needed back home. And I miss my family."

"The time for you to live in Koinopia is not now," Jasper assured him. "A true Valenian must first battle for victory on the Earth."

"And there's still some battles to win," Matt said.

Ryan elbowed Matt's ribs. "Could we just get back? Before my mom discovers I *haven't* been at basketball camp for the last week?

Matt turned to Jasper. "I'll see you soon?" He reached into his jeans and pulled out the sixth ruby.

"Trust the timing." Jasper's eyes twinkled.

Matt picked up the chest and placed the sixth ruby on top. He slapped his thigh, signaling Wrinkles. His dog barked and jumped into his arms. Ryan drew closer.

Dawdle's head popped up from the stream. He'd made it to Koinopia through the river. "I thank you, my friends!" He sputtered out water. "Goodbye!"

Ryan and Matt laughed.

"Ready?" Matt asked.

"Let's do it!" Ryan said.

Matt lifted the golden latch and opened the red chest.

HOMEWARD

A puffy cloud escaped the chest, forming a dome over Matt and Ryan. Below them, a smooth sheet of golden glass descended downward.

"Uh-oh," Matt said. He started forward but slipped from his feet and started sliding down the glassy surface like he was riding a rollercoaster. Matt held Wrinkles tight.

Ryan slid and zoomed beside him, his cheeks flapping as they plunged down, then shot upward into the blue sky and clouds. Rainbows streaked ahead of them, and they glided onto the arcs—one arc, two, three. They shot off the top of the last rainbow into the stars, and everything went dark. Matt closed his eyes. It felt awesome, and he didn't want the ride to end.

But then he *bump, bump, bumped* onto a rough surface. Matt opened his eyes. He and Ryan had landed on top of his garage at home and bounced down the roof.

They dropped off the side of the roof and landed on the canvas top of Grandpa's Jeep. The canvas gave way, catching them like a baseball mitt. The red chest plunked down beside them. A cloud of dust puffed up, and Matt smelled dirt. He coughed.

Ryan looked over, wide-eyed. "I think we're back." He grinned wide and stretched his arms.

"No doubt about it." Matt felt as if he'd just awakened from a dream. He rubbed his hip, then shook his arms and legs. Everything seemed to be cool. "Let's get down from here."

Wrinkles barked. He escaped Matt's arms, jumped down from the canvas onto the front of the jeep, then hit the ground.

"Did I just hear a bark?" Mom's voice floated to Matt from in front of the garage.

"Hurry!" Matt slid off the canvas, dropped to the ground, and hid the red chest behind a bush. Ryan followed.

Mom appeared in the sideyard where they stood. Dad came into view.

"Matt?" Mom swept forward and hugged him. "Thank God you're okay!"

Dad strode over and gripped Matt's shoulder. "Where have you been?"

"Um—" Matt thought quick. He'd last seen his parents six hours ago, in Earth-time. Matt had promised to text but didn't. He was in trouble.

"I found Wrinkles, Mom!"

A smile spread on Mom's face, and her eyes lit up. "Oh, Wrinkles. We thought we'd lost you! Here, boy!"

Wrinkles ran to Mom and she swept him into a hug.

Dad rubbed Wrinkles's back. "Buddy, where have you been?"

Matt was temporarily out of trouble. Wrinkles had distracted his parents.

The back door of the house opened, and Grandpa came out. "What's all this commotion?"

"Matt's back! And so is Wrinkles!" Mom said.

"Son! You almost gave me a heart attack. And where'd you find that ugly mug?" Grandpa shook his head.

Dad wasn't distracted long. "So what's the story?"

"You wouldn't believe where we found Wrinkles," Matt said.

"Try me."

"It was a ways off, Mr. Silvers," Ryan began.

"I thought you were at camp," Dad said.

"I just got back to Baywood," Ryan said. "Would you believe Wrinkles followed me?"

"To camp?" Mom said.

"Uh," Ryan said. Sweat beaded out on his forehead.

"All the way to Coach's house?" Dad asked.

"He followed me outside of Baywood," Ryan said.

"Cell service out at Coach's place is sketchy," Dad turned to Matt. "Is that why you didn't text?"

"I would have called if I could have," Matt said.

Dad nodded. "I'm just glad you're back safe. All of you."

◇◇◇◇◇◇

Ryan found his four-wheeler in the bushes where Julie had rolled it. He fired it up and smoke blew out the back. The exhaust made him cough as he gave it some gas. Ryan zoomed through Matt's backyard to the neighborhood trail. Dusk settled around the woods on his right. On the left, lights shone through the windows as he passed behind neighborhood houses.

He emerged from the trail on a path that ran beside his house. A truck rumbled down the street and came into view. Ryan stopped. It was Coach's truck! Coach and the team had just returned from camp!

The truck lights lit the path where Ryan sat and slowed as it approached. Through the front windshield, Coach's brow wrinkled, and he wheeled to the shoulder of the road and stopped.

I'm busted.

The passenger side window rolled down.

"Ryan? Is that you?" Coach bellowed across the seat.

Ryan nodded and tried to smile.

"We had awesome practices at camp," Coach said.

"Yeah!" Some guys chimed in from the back seat.

Caleb sat next to the window. "And Coach got shaving cream on his pillow!" he joked.

"But nobody knows who did it!" Colin said from the middle spot in front. All the guys laughed.

"Yeah, yeah." Coach said and shook his head. "When I didn't get your permission slip, I realized your parents must have changed their minds about letting you come," Coach said.

"I've had things going on," Ryan answered.

"Okay, I get it," Coach said. "The high school coach can drill you on the new plays next fall."

Ryan nodded. "Yeah."

Coach nodded and Caleb rolled up the window. They pulled back onto the street and drove off. Ryan gave them a final wave and zoomed across the yard to his garage.

That was a close call.

"Ryan!" Chloe spotted him from the other side of the garage. She bounded off her mini-trampoline into the yard. Mom and Dad sat around the fire pit, watching her.

His parents turned when they heard the four-wheeler. They met him as he rumbled near.

"Ryan!" Mom smiled. "So glad you're back!"

"Hey, son!" Dad said. "We missed you. How was camp?"

Ryan braked. "Coach said the practices were awesome." He nodded and rolled past them into the garage.

He parked and switched off the engine. The quiet surrounding him gave him peace. He got off the four-wheeler and grabbed his camp bag. How would he explain the clean clothes to Mom? He'd think of something. Right now, there was only one thing that mattered.

He was finally home.

CHAPTER THIRTY-TWO

HISS

Matt paced in his baseball team's dugout and checked the scoreboard. The Baywood Hawks trailed by three runs. His team's last chance to score loomed ahead, and they'd already made two outs.

Why did the first game of the season have to be against their annoying rivals, the Westside Warriors?

"Hey, Silvers," Wesley said. "Hope you get lucky and we beat Westside again. Just like in basketball."

"Luck had nothing to do with it, Wesley," Lucas spoke up.

Needles sat at the score table, eating a hamburger. "Might as well let the pitcher hit you, Silvers. It's the only way you'll get on base."

Matt shook his head and walked off. A whiff of hamburger floated to him from the concession stand. He could stand something to eat too, but he had to stay focused.

Baywood had beaten Westside for the basketball championship only a few weeks ago. Matt's last-second shot had defeated them. And Westside wanted revenge. Badly.

Now the same guys who'd played on Westside's basketball team faced Matt on the baseball field. Logan Myerson, who'd trounced Matt's ankle during the basketball game, now pitched from the mound. And Brock Griffin, who'd bullied under the basket, crouched behind home plate as the catcher.

Matt's team trailed by three runs, but Caleb had a hit and stood on first base. Two guys waited in the lineup ahead of Matt—Parker, then Colin. After them, Matt would be batting, facing Logan's pitches.

It was bad enough playing Westside, but Matt also had to watch out for Wesley. Matt remembered Wesley's threat from the week before spring break.

Wait 'til you need help, Silvers. I'll be the one laughing then.

What would Wesley do? Matt hoped Wesley's good side would prevail instead of the snarky one.

Parker stood next to home base as Logan rocketed a pitch right down the middle. Parker didn't swing.

"Strike!" the umpire called.

Another fastball sailed over the plate, but this time, Parker smacked the ball hard into right field. The ball bounced twice before the outfielder caught it and shot it to first base. Parker slid into first, beating the throw. Caleb advanced to second.

Colin adjusted his helmet and strode to home plate, ready to face Logan's pitches.

"Silvers!" Coach hollered. "You're on deck!"

Matt pulled on his helmet and searched for his bat. It lay in a corner of the dugout, partly behind the bench. He hurried over and lifted the bat out of the dirt.

A black-striped lizard looked Matt straight in the eye. The green creature sat atop his bat, and its claws gripped it like a vise. Some kind of pouch puffed up under its chin.

Matt dropped the bat. His heart leaped in his chest, and he backed away.

A Skink?

Julie had told him they'd run off the Skinks with ice and peacock feathers. Hadn't all the Skinks disappeared into the dark water of the whirlpool, vanquished to the Dark Void?

Guess not.

This Skink's tail curled behind it in a swirl. It gaped and a hiss escaped through its lizard teeth.

"Matt!" Wesley snapped. "Hurry up and get on deck!"

"Don't have a bat!" Matt sputtered. No one else had seen the Skink. Matt wouldn't antagonize it. The thing looked ready to bite him.

A black bird swept into the dugout. *Starling?*

"*ACK!*" Starling bared his beak.

"Silvers! Get on deck!" Coach bellowed again.

"Something wrong with your bat?" Wesley chided. "Guess you can use this one." He tossed Matt a hefty bat. Matt caught it and headed for the warm-up circle. It weighed heavy in his hands and looked too long.

Colin smacked a single, sending Parker to second and Caleb to third.

The whole scenario played out just as Matt had envisioned it the night before—bases loaded, two outs, and his team trailed by three. And Matt's turn to bat came next.

Sometimes, his beyond-seeing didn't seem like a good thing.

The game's outcome now rested on Matt's shoulders. If he made an out, Westside had the win. But if Matt got on base, Lucas was the next batter and might hit a homer with the bases loaded.

Matt steeled himself and headed for the batter's box. He planted his feet beside home plate, lifted the heavy bat behind him, and bent his knees. Matt turned his head to face Logan straight-on. The field lights blazed onto the diamond, and Matt's eyes watered. He blinked them back and focused.

Logan smirked and glanced at Brock.

Matt didn't move from his stance. Logan peered at Matt, glove in front and leaning forward. He wound up and released the ball. It shot right down the middle. Matt had to take it.

He swung the bat, and his wrist wavered, making the swing uneven. He missed the ball!

Hoots and claps came from the Westside crowd.

Beads of sweat gathered on Matt's forehead. He stepped out of the box, wiped his brow, and straightened his helmet. Mom and Dad clapped from behind the fence. Wrinkles had settled in the grass nearby, and Grandpa sat in a lawn chair holding Wrinkles's leash.

"Make it your ball!" Dad shouted.

"Hey, batter, batter, batter . . ." the Westside dugout chanted.

"Those sassy pants think they've got you," Grandpa said. "But you'll show 'em."

Logan stared at Matt from the mound. Was he trying to intimidate? It didn't work.

Matt wasn't afraid. Logan finally released the ball.

Milliseconds ticked away as the ball came straight over the plate—again! Matt zeroed in and swung. The heavy bat came around and connected.

The ball made contact with the middle of the bat and landed between the pitcher's mound and third base. *Oh no!*

Logan scrambled for the ball as Matt raced to first. The first baseman tried to block him, but Matt ran and slammed onto first base without a tag.

The play is at home plate.

Matt turned. Logan must have bobbled the ball because Caleb kept sprinting forward, only two steps away from scoring a run. Logan zipped the ball to Brock. It went over his head and hit the backstop.

Not only was Caleb safe, but Parker ran for home plate. Brock finally grabbed the ball and tried to beat Parker to home base for a tag—but too late.

Another run for the Hawks!

Brock launched the ball to the third baseman, trying to get Colin out. The baseman caught the ball and raced for Colin, trying to tag his back as he ran toward home.

"*ACK! ACK! ACK!*" Squawks came from the dugout.

As Matt sprinted to third after Colin, a green flash caught his eye. The Skink was heading for the field! Starling had chased it out!

Wrinkles growled and barked, straining ahead. Grandpa almost turned over in his chair as Wrinkles pulled free. Matt's dog raced after the lizard and shot around the fence, running between the third baseman and Colin. Wrinkles's leash trailed behind him and tripped the Westside player!

Colin made it safely home and Matt was on third. Would the ump call them back?

The crowd that had clapped and shouted before became silent, then broke out into laughter.

The bobble, the overthrow, the squawking and barking, the weird lizard, the trailing leash, and the third baseman's tumble. It was too much. The players began laughing too—even Wesley. It was like Baseball Bloopers and Blunders!

The ump stopped the game and called the coaches over. After everyone calmed down and the animals were rounded up, a decision had been made.

Colin would return to third and Matt to second. Matt couldn't believe he had a double from that short hit, but his team still trailed by one run!

But it was Lucas's turn to bat. He'd warmed up while the ump and coaches met. He took his stance next to home plate and held his bat high.

Logan eyed the tall seventh-grader and sent a fastball low over the plate.

"Strike!" the umpire called.

Lucas's shoulders sank, and he glanced at the dugout.

Coach gave him a thumbs-up and clapped. "Way to hang in there. This one's yours!"

"You can do it, Lucas!" Matt called from second base.

The next pitch was high but over the plate. Lucas took it and popped the ball high behind him. It sailed over the backstop.

"Heads up!" a few parents shouted. The ball hit the scoretable, smashed the hamburger, bounced up, and hit Needles on the nose.

"Ow!" Needles grabbed his nose.

Matt gaped. *Could the game get any weirder?*

Lucas had two strikes, so this was it. Logan took his time kicking dirt around, delaying the game. He finally threw the last pitch, and Lucas hit a line drive right at the pitcher's knee!

Logan howled but scooped up the ball and sent it home. Too late! Colin scored the tying run, and Lucas made it to first. Matt scurried to third. Would he have a chance to score the winning run?

Wyatt's turn came next. As he started for the batter's box, Julie and her high school girlfriends waved to him from the bleachers.

He hesitated and tipped up his head at them, a lazy smile on his face.

Matt fumed. Wyatt should just concentrate on the game.

Matt guessed Wyatt had a thing for Julie. After all, he'd helped her run off the Skinks, and they'd spent all that time together in the library.

But did *she* like *him*?

Wyatt stood beside the plate, and Logan wound up. The next pitch came straight over the plate. *Crack!*

Wyatt sent the ball over third, just above Matt's head. Matt sped toward home! He would score the winning run! He stomped onto home base and ran past, then turned to look behind him.

Where was the ball? It rolled slowly along the baseline in left field. It was rolling out-of-bounds!

The outfielders must have thought so too, because they didn't scoop it up to put it into play. The ball rolled slowly along the white line and . . . stopped. Firmly on the line, but not out!

The ball had stayed in bounds. Matt's run counted, and Baywood won the game!

Matt spied Ryan behind the fence, just down from his parents. He met Matt as he exited the field.

"Good game." He gave him a five. "But weird."

"Tell me about it." Matt took off his cap and fanned his head. "What happened to that Skink anyway?"

"Wasn't a Skink," Ryan said. "Look—" He nodded toward Baywood's dugout. Wesley held the lizard in his hand, scooted it down into his bag, and zipped it up.

"That was Wesley's pet chameleon?"

"Truth," Ryan said.

Matt shook his head. "He must have put that lizard on my bat, trying to scare me or something."

"Did it?" Ryan laughed.

"Well, yeah!" Matt laughed too. "Did you see that thing?"

"Ugly."

"Yep."

Julie and her friends filed down from the bleachers. She'd probably come over to congratulate him.

Matt looked up as she came near, but she walked past him. Wyatt stood a few feet away.

"Wyatt, good hit!" Julie said.

Matt cringed.

Needles and Wesley came toward them. Needles held a tissue to his nose.

"Saw you laughing, Wes," Matt said. "But in a good way."

"Yeah, whatever." Wes rolled his eyes. "Weirdest game ever."

"Wonder why?" Ryan said. "Wouldn't have anything to do with that lizard of yours, would it?"

Needles bumped Matt on purpose as he walked by. "You might have won the game." Needles snorted through his bungled nostrils. "But I think you lost your girlfriend."

Matt shrugged him off with his elbow. "She's not my..." Matt started, but stopped when he saw Julie gazing over at him.

"We're friends," Matt said.

Wrinkles bounded over and Matt knelt to pet him. His parents and Grandpa followed over to congratulate him.

"Way to turn the game around," Dad said.

"I didn't have a great hit, but maybe it was enough," Matt said.

"That's all that's expected," Grandpa said. "Do what you can, when you can."

Mom bent to pet Wrinkles. "And keep your friends close by."

EPILOGUE

A gentle breeze skimmed over the cresting waves of the Living Waters. Jasper sat on Torch as his golden steed ambled along the crystalline beach.

Koinopia, I have missed you!

Prism colors winked upon the shimmering sea. A golden light, brighter than anything on Earth, filled the country with life. A swirl of pastel Butterlings swept around them and danced along the wind before soaring into the sky.

A happy peace engulfed Jasper as he inhaled the freshness of luscious fruits and fragrant plants. Berry and melon, peach and apple, a little lemon—all blended with honeysuckle and lilac in a bouquet of invigorating scent.

It is good to be home.

As he passed through the Woodlands, cedar, pine, cinnamon, and frankincense infused his senses. How he'd missed the forest creatures! His friends of wing, hoof, and paw—adorned in soft fur and vibrant feathers—surrounded him in a welcoming host.

He touched Torch with his heels and guided him through the forest, across meadows, and to a cliff next to a waterfall. Mist settled upon Jasper's cheek as the flowing water crashed below. Matt, Julie, and Ryan had treaded above this stream only weeks before. The journey had taught them to step out and trust.

"Forward, Torch!" Jasper commanded, and his horse galloped on. Rolling mountains appeared, and soft, falling snow touched Jasper's shoulders as they wound through the hills. Peppermint filled his senses. His eyes swept over the sculpted mounds and softened trees as Torch padded and crunched through the snowy paradise.

The sharp peaks in the distance drew Jasper's gaze—tall mountains of flame and shadow where the Stones of Fire had been forged. Soon, Jasper would scale the peaks and return the Stones to the mountain flames and the rocks that glowed with molten heat.

He turned Torch onto the upward path. Those drawn to Koinopia would travel the same way and endure many trials. Their journey would lead them through the sharp mountains, not around them.

Jasper's heart melted when he thought of Matt. Difficult tests awaited him. Would he endure?

One ruby and a final scroll of wisdom remained to guide Matt. He must learn to choose wisdom, even when his natural impulses might turn him in another direction.

Matt's next choices would decide the final outcome of his calling. Would he triumph as a Valenian?

○○○○○○

Principal Harris stood beside the entrance doors of Baywood Junior High, greeting the students returning from spring break.

"Hello."

"Welcome back."

"Make this a good one."

The kids streamed in from buses and drop-off zones, carrying bags, notebooks, purses, and backpacks. Some looked tanned from vacation and wore shorts. Others had on jeans and T-shirts. Some eighth-grade girls had upswept buns, and many wore makeup.

The warm, spring wind breezed into the hallway. Gone were the dark mornings and wet sidewalks of winter. The students looked positive and rested after their break.

"Hi, Mr. Harris." Matt Silvers nodded as he and Ryan Davis walked by. It amazed the principal—how the two had matured in the last year.

A clique of students checked out Wyatt Sawyer as he strolled into the school. And Julie Spencer walked alongside him. Hmm, what was that about?

Buzzz!

The tone sounded, signaling the transition to the first period. A groan arose from the commons area as the students headed for class. They called to one another as they walked past him.

"Where you headed?

"Wait up!"

"Where's my notebook?"

They all dispersed peacefully, but Mr. Harris would check for stragglers after the bell. Fifteen minutes later, he walked the quiet halls and peeked into classrooms through the door glass.

An acrid smell sickened his stomach. Had the science classes already started their experiments? He strolled faster to the science hallway.

Mrs. Grant whipped open her classroom door. "Quickly students! Out this way!" A hand rested above her mouth. "Oh—Mr. Harris! There's a fire in the lab! Someone threw a vape into the trash can! The paper towels caught fire!"

The principal's head throbbed and his heart quickened. "Everyone out!" He scrambled to the wall and pulled the red fire alarm, then ran to open every hallway door. "Out—follow the emergency exit! Quickly! Stay calm!"

Whoop! Whoop! Whoop! Whoop! The alarm sounded, along with flashing lights and a continuous bell.

Students streamed out into halls. Some girls screamed, and a few tripped.

"Did all the students get out of your classroom?" the principal asked Mrs. Grant.

"Yes, I checked my attendance. Matt Silvers tried to help me, then smoke billowed into the room, and I couldn't see. I think he went out the side classroom door."

"Sure he got out ?" Mr. Harris asked as he raised his cell to call the fire department.

"I don't know . . ." Tears formed in the teacher's eyes.

○○○○○○

Matt coughed, black smoke clouding his vision. Now, where was the door? He felt over the shelves and desks at the side of the room. He glimpsed the door leading outside, just a few steps away. He hurried forward but smacked into something tall, muscled, and hairy. He couldn't see its face. The thing wouldn't move out of his way. He shuffled left, and the creature moved left. He moved to the right, and it blocked his escape! The smoke grew thicker, and Matt knelt on the floor.

Was it a Wolvin? Had it entered Baywood for revenge because of Jasper's escape?

The thing bellowed loud and long—it wasn't a Wolvin howl. The roar in Matt's ears sounded primitive and terrifying. A paw and long claws swept in front of Matt, just missing his face.

A figure crowded between Matt and the creature. A coat of mail swung over two muscled legs.

"Run, Matt Silvers!"

A mace swung and struck the creature's head. The bawling animal wavered. Matt sprang to his feet and darted around it to the door. He shoved down the lever and it popped open. Fresh air flowed into his nostrils, and he fled outside.

Matt ran away from the building and collapsed. His vision shrank to a tunnel.

Ryan's voice called to him. "Matt, can you hear me? Are you still with us?"

IN APPRECIATION

Thank you to everyone who has given me inspiration and support on this writing journey.

To my parents, husband, children, and grandchildren, I say thanks for the beautiful memories. I have been blessed to share life with you!

Much appreciation to my friends from wonderful writers' groups—Southern Christian Writers, Byhalia Christian Writers, Kentucky Christian Writers, and Blue Ridge Mountain Christian Writers. Thank you for your support, encouragement, and love along the way.

Thank you to my editorial colleagues in this series, editors Victoria Sherrow and Amanda Varian; interior designers Lisa Parnell and Ken Raney.

Many thanks to my very talented illustrators in this series, Brandon Dorman and Joel Cockrell.

No woman is an island! I could not have written these books without God's help and the friends He has sent my way.

Thanks to God, most of all, for blessing me with the inspiration to write and surrounding me with great people. "And we know that all things work together for good to them that love God, to them who are the called according to his purpose." (Romans 8:28, KJV)

My thanks and best wishes to my young readers, their parents, and grandparents—may God bless you with His very best!